It's All
Downhill

David Ward

To Liz, Matthew and Chloe.

Acknowledgements

Thanks and gratitude to my wife Liz, for her patience and forbearance when I disappear to write for hours on end.

To Nigel Peake for kindly agreeing to provide the excellent cover design and illustrations.

To Janie McIlroy for the speed and precision of her proof reading and her tireless quest to remove my commas.

I must mention all those involved in the Deloitte Ride Across Britain and in particular Threshold Sports and their magnificent team whose organisation and friendliness make a tough event bearable and almost enjoyable!

Many thanks to The Writer's Workshop and in particular Debi Alper, for their guidance and realistic feedback on my writing.

Finally, thanks to my biking mates, Tony, Peter, Simon and Matthew for always waiting for me and picking me up and dusting me off when I fall off.

Day Minus One

Morning....

Men don't normally buy moist sanitary wipes, least of all from a chemist in an airport terminal. The man two ahead of me in the checkout queue has four packets in his hand. I look at my single packet and panic. The list of things to pack hadn't defined quantity and if I'm honest, I have no precise idea of what to use them for. The packet says it contains forty wipes, which over nine days works out at four or five wipes a day, which by applying a few varied uses, seems more than enough. I can't begin to imagine what bodily functions necessitate four times that amount, yet feel unsettled. Perhaps the man has done the ride before, perhaps the number of moist sanitary wipes is the key to success or failure.

Nine days, nearly a thousand miles - one end of the country to the other on a bike. The thought scares the shit out of me, but that's why I'm doing it. Something to pull me out of the maudlin world that I've drifted into after the divorce. Along with five hundred or so other people, I'm about to '*face a challenge of a lifetime*' and test the organisers' evangelical mantra, '*Find Yourself - There's More There*'. I'd been told about the Haskin Long Britain Ride by one of my clients who holds some kind of non-executive directorship with Haskin, who are one of those accounting conglomerates who believe that they rule the world. No doubt this is their way to be seen supporting human endeavour and raising thousands of pounds for worthy causes. Maybe it's a way of assuaging their guilt for the excesses of the day job, which is something I know all about. *She* works for Haskin's biggest competitor and for eight years I'd been suffocated by the collateral fall-out of corporate bullshit.

Running a marathon had always appealed to me, but only the idea, I hate running. The ride seemed like a good alternative. I've always liked bikes, they're mechanical and efficient and unlike running, your energy is converted into something greater than the effort you put in. I hadn't ridden a bike for years, my love affair with *her* and four wheels meant that I had no time for two wheels, but after the divorce, time was something I suddenly had a lot of.

The man with the moist wipes has paid for them and walks past me. He looks like a cyclist, his tanned face has panda-like white patches over his eyes and no doubt his upper arms and thighs have the telltale contrast of dark brown and ghostly white where the shorts and jersey end. As I leave the shop I search him out, feeling the need to talk to someone. He's in a coffee shop and I sit at the table next to him.

"Are you doing the ride?" I ask.

It could have been a ridiculous question, but he answers as if it was totally normal.

"Yes.. Bob."

He answers with such assertiveness that I struggle to overcome a compulsion to duck my head. He holds out his hand. His handshake is warm and clammy.

"Mark," I answer.

"Mark, good to meet you. Which club?"

"Sorry?"

"Cycling club, who do you ride with?"

"I don't belong to a club."

Our conversation grinds on slowly. Bob works for Haskin and he pompously tells me that he's a partner. I'm not impressed, these firms have so many partners that if they put all their names on the notepaper, you'd turn over two pages before knowing what the letter was about. I want to avoid admitting that I know anything about his world, but fail and inwardly curse that I still use *her* reflected glory.

"My ex-wife works for Dubois, she's a partner in mergers and acquisitions."

Bob gives an expression of approval. Suddenly I'm interesting. "Oh, she's at the sharp end and what do you do?" he asks.

How I hate that question.

"I'm in motorsport," I reply.

It's a fudged answer, but sounds better than saying I'm a race driver without any sponsors who makes a living buying and selling cars. Nine times out of ten it's an answer that falls to the floor, leaving the person asking floundering for a reply. This time I'm grateful it does just that.

Bob gestures towards a man walking past. The man is quite short and his torso is as thin as a stick insect, yet his thighs and calves bulge with muscle. He's also wearing Lycra cycling clothes.

"He looks like he's doing it."

I recognise the man. "Yes, that's Lawrence. Haven't you followed the Facebook page?"

Bob frowns. "No, I don't have time for all that stuff."

Haskin had set up a Facebook page and invited riders to post anecdotes about their training and preparations. I'd posted once, an honest account of my struggle to get fit and which was met with stony silence. I quickly realised that the page was a conduit only for the successes of people's training - the killer one hundred miles across mountain ranges with gradients that would challenge a mountain goat and all with a sack of coal on your back. Lawrence had revelled in posting, there was nothing he couldn't do. He'd put a picture of himself on the page and apologised that he was wearing a suit, explaining that he was a lawyer. He'd said that he wouldn't look like that on the ride, but he looks exactly the same. Take away the suit and add Lycra and he still looks a prat.

"Finchley Road," Bob says.

Why the hell does he keep opening conversations with ambiguous statements?

"Pardon," I reply.

"Finchley Road Club - the jersey." Bob nods towards Lawrence.

"But why's he wearing it now?" I ask. "We don't start until tomorrow."

The absurdity of Lawrence wearing full cycling kit for the journey to John O'Groats doesn't seem to register with Bob. It's perhaps no more ridiculous than a coach load of football supporters at the motorway services, all wearing facsimiles of their team's kit. Maybe Lawrence is less absurd. At least he'd be taking part and not merely spectating.

I glance up at the departures monitor. *Shit!* The nine o'clock flight to Inverness is delayed.

Afternoon....

It's two o'clock and there's still no sign of the coach to take us to John O'Groats. By some form of osmosis, word filters through that the coach has been delayed at Edinburgh due to a late flight. For some reason I feel lonely, which is ridiculous. I've been on my own for eighteen months and wouldn't say that I've been lonely, more in a vacuum of nothingness. No highs and no lows. Maybe I'm feeling like this because I thought the ride would be instantly uplifting, but it's hard to find anything uplifting about standing in an empty coach park enveloped in grey dank drizzle.

Perhaps I thought that I would instantly bond with my fellow riders. There are about twenty of us waiting for the coach. Most are around my age or a little older and a couple look to be in their fifties or maybe sixties, their faces lean and weather-beaten from years of cycling. With the exception of Bob and Lawrence nobody is talking. I could join them, but can't be bothered. Bob isn't going to be the 'special friend for life' that the ride organisers had promised I'd find. By the time the flight had left, our conversation had totally stalled and I was grateful when he'd joined the priority boarding queue whilst I waited in steerage. I don't actually need to move in order to hear Bob. Why the hell do some people feel the need to shout when having a normal conversation? Is he deaf? Somehow I doubt that he is. I have a theory that it's all to do with private education. I'm pretty sure that Bob is a product of a public school. I think that the children at these schools have to talk loudly to get themselves noticed. The result is a spiraling increase in volume until everybody is shouting at the top of their voice just to be heard. Bob is shouting about corporate law and Lawrence is nodding sagely whilst peering over his horn rimmed glasses. Lawrence was never going to be that special friend. As soon as I learned he was a lawyer that was it. I've had a basinful of lawyers.

The coach is a double-decker with facing seats and tables. The man sitting opposite smiles as I settle into my seat. I don't mean to sound unkind, but this man is old. He's not like the other older men, his face is not lean, it's podgy and red as opposed to brown, his hair is not tightly cropped, but wispy grey. Christ, he can't be doing the ride.

He leans forward and holds out his hand.

"Hello, I'm Mike, I've been on this bloody coach for six hours already. We sat at Edinburgh Airport for nearly three hours."

I introduce myself and make small talk about the delays, desperately wanting to find out if he's doing the ride, but not being able to find a way of asking. Mike then answers my question. The rain is now heavy and he gestures at the window.

"I hope the weather improves by tomorrow. I hate riding in the rain," he says.

"So how's the training gone, are you feeling fit?" I ask, trying not to sound incredulous.

"Well I turned seventy this year, so I didn't want to overdo things. I did a few fifty milers with a couple of friends who are in a cycling club."

"So you've been cycling for years?"

Mike smiles. "No, just fancied doing the ride. Another box to tick since the wife's been gone. I've climbed Kilimanjaro, been through the desert in Jordan, been to New York."

"I'm sorry," I say.

"Sorry?"

"About your wife."

He laughs. "Don't be, I should have got rid of her years ago. Why I waited until I was sixty seven before I divorced her, I'll never know."

I tell him about my divorce and he congratulates me.

The three hour journey to John O'Groats was going to be my opportunity to take in a bit of the Highland scenery. I've only been to Scotland once before - Glasgow for a stag weekend, but it could have been anywhere. Somewhere with pubs, bars and a claustrophobic shared hotel room. I'm discounting the next four days when I'll ride the length of Scotland. My training rides having proved that when cycling, you don't see much of the surrounding countryside. Your attention needs to be fixed on the road twenty feet ahead in order to spot crater like potholes, which if ridden into, at best puncture your tyre and at worst, catapult you towards a very hard meeting with the road.

I nod mechanically to Mike. Since we left Inverness, I have looked at Mike and nodded and looked out of the window and nodded. I realise that as long as I nod, Mike will continue with his life story. He's distracting, but not boring. His story confirms a spirit that's been able to totally redefine his life at a time when most are worrying about how they can pay for the care home. He was a sergeant in the Met traffic police until he retired at fifty and then ran a guest house in

Illfracombe. The guest house is up for sale which he hopes will, with his police pension, provide enough money to fund his new-found lifestyle and his ex-wife's dotage.

"Sex is brilliant. I've never had so much. That Internet is marvellous," Mike says.

I keep looking out of the window - I really don't want to have this conversation. Not only has this seventy year old man sailed happily through a divorce and is confidently embarking on a challenge that scares the life out of me, BUT he's also having sex. I don't do women any more, let alone sex. Eight years with the same woman has left me with the firm belief that I wouldn't know where to start all over again.

We drive through Golspie, a well ordered town or is it a village? Pretty stone houses with immaculate gardens and a castle. It strikes me as a Scottish Portmeirion, almost surreal, too perfect. Surely people can't live here in the middle of nowhere, earn money and take part in the real world.

On my right is the sea, but my view is suddenly obscured by a black 4x4 passing the coach in the same direction. My instincts tell me that this isn't a road for overtaking.

The coach's brakes force me back into my seat. Bags, water bottles, everything in the shelf above are thrown forward and shower onto the seats and gangway.

Mike shoots forward. He tries to stop himself with his feet, but they slip and he slides under the table, his chin glancing the edge as he collapses beneath it.

The coach shudders to a stop.

I crane my neck to look out of the windscreen and see the 4x4 speeding away, apparently oblivious to the carnage that he could have caused.

Mike struggles to drag himself back from underneath the table. His chin is bleeding.

"What the hell happened?" he asks.

"Some prat overtook and we had to brake hard. Are you okay? You've cut your chin."

He puts his hand to his chin and immediately takes it away, staring at the blood covering his fingers. I delve into an old sandwich bag, retrieve a paper serviette and hand it to him. He holds it tight to his face, but I see a red stain spreading through the paper. Mike's ruddy complexion has vanished, he looks grey and his bottom lip is beginning to quiver. He suddenly looks all of his seventy years.

The coach driver pulls over into a lay-by, gets out of his seat and walks along the gangway asking if everyone is alright and re-stowing bags in the overhead shelf. Mike turns his head away towards the window. I suspect that he doesn't want to make a fuss, but the driver notices the blood which is now oozing out of the serviette and running down Mike's arm. I explain to the driver what happened. Mike is still looking out of the window.

"You didn't have your seat belt on, did you? Didn't you hear the safety announcement - read the signs?" He gesticulates at the signs riveted on the back of each seat.

The driver's voice is patronising, as if he were talking to a child or an idiot. Mike doesn't reply and I'm compelled to answer.

"Okay, he should have, but I'm sure he won't sue you or the company."

Mike turns his head and nods sheepishly. The driver looks unconvinced.

A voice booms, Bob has decided to stick his oar in. "He's going to need that looked at. Stitches for certain. Is there a hospital nearby?"

The driver grunts, "Wick," then shuffles back down the gangway.

Mike smiles weakly. "That's a bloody good start."

I'm tempted to make a joke about his choice of words, but decide not to.

Caithness General Hospital in Wick looks like the rest of Wick, deserted. A weathered finger sign points towards the A&E department. The coach stops and the driver opens the front door, but remains seated and silent. He's done his bit.

Mike looks at me.

What do I do? I *should* probably go with him, but God knows how long it will take and we're already three hours later than we should be.

"Mike, go and get yourself sorted out. I'll get your bags off at John O'Groats and explain what's happened. You can get a taxi, it's not far."

The look - a seventy year old child. I feel bad.

He gathers his stuff together. I think about giving him my mobile number, but decide against it. I'll sort out his luggage and make sure the organisers know what's happened. That's enough.

As Mike gets off the coach, a sudden squall forces the heavy rain almost horizontally across the car park. The coach driver immediately moves off, leaving Mike soaked, alone and still pressing the saturated serviette into his chin.

The coach crawls around the hospital's one way system and finally reaches the junction with the main road, where it waits for a small convoy to pass. There are two liveried estate cars, their roofs piled high with racing bikes, two vans and two massive motorhomes. I've seen a lot of motorhomes at motor racing circuits, but nothing as impressive as these.

"Trans-Global."

It sounds like a public address system. Bob isn't talking to anybody in particular and looks around to gauge reaction. Our eyes meet and he obviously senses that I have no idea what he's talking about.

" Trans-Global," he repeats, as if repetition will make me understand. My face obviously remains blank. He tries again, but adds detail this time.

"They're the Trans-Global cycling team. Russian. Owned by a guy who's a billionaire. He's trying to do an Abramovich by spending millions setting up a cycling team. He says they'll win the Tour de France in two years."

"So what are they doing here?" I ask. "They're surely not doing the ride."

"They might well be using it for training. There are some good riders in the elite riders group," Bob answers.

I think about the contrast between the super fit professional riders sitting in their luxury motorhomes ahead of us and Mike sitting in casualty with a paper serviette pressed to his face. This ride is certainly going to be a strange affair.

Fifteen minutes later we turn inland and the landscape turns flatter and more drab. The signs begin to point to John O'Groats. We're on a long straight road and across the fields I catch sight of the Haskin Long Britain Ride Base Camp. Slowly it comes into focus and all I can see is row upon row of green and blue tents. My heart sinks. I'd never been convinced that camping for nine nights would work for me, I'm more of a four star hotel room man, something which *she'd* nurtured during our time together. Through the rain, the camp reminds me of the refugee camps you see on the news after some civil war, or something hastily erected to house the victims of floods or earthquakes.

Evening....

The girls on the registration desk are doing their best, but the layout of the marquee hadn't been designed for rain and only about three people can queue in the dry with everyone else being forced to huddle outside and get soaked. I explain about Mike and they try to give me his registration stuff. I over-protest my lack of responsibility - *I don't really know him... I met him for the first time on the coach..........I'm just doing him a favour by bringing his bag.*

Their efforts to speed up registration creates an overload of information. The entrant's pass that I must wear at all times is hanging around my neck on a lanyard and I've stuffed the large envelope containing written instructions into my jacket pocket. I can't remember half of what I've been told, but the girl's insistence that it is all written down in the envelope is reassuring.

I need to find my bike which has been brought up to John O'Groats by lorry. The bikes are stored in compounds and I've got to remove the foam taped to it for protection and fix the pedals and handlebars. The compounds are past the entrance to the camp which is now deserted apart from a solitary security guard who is standing by the large blue inflatable start gantry which reminds me of a bouncy castle. No doubt security is needed in case someone in the area is having a children's party and takes a fancy to it. To the left, the road leads down to the centre of John O'Groats, which from what I can see, doesn't amount to much and to the right, the road is straight and flat and in the distance I can make out a solitary pub, a B&B and a few houses.

The rain has now been joined by a howling gale. Christ this is a desolate place.

I need to hurry. There's a briefing meeting in half an hour and I still have to eat. I've had nothing more than a bowl of cereal, a chocolate croissant, a sandwich and a bag of crisps since I got up. I'm cycling over one hundred miles tomorrow and remember the message of every piece of training advice that I've read over the last six months - you MUST load with carbohydrates. Load! I've had less to eat today than I would if I was spending tomorrow in bed.

Tents are pitched everywhere and all I can hear above the din of the wind is the frantic flapping of tent fabric and the shouting of groups of men desperately trying to pin tents down before they fly away to the Orkneys. Is there such a thing as a refugee camp for the refugees of a refugee camp? If there is, it's highly likely to land in the Orkneys sometime tomorrow.

The bike compounds are massive. Row upon row of horizontal bars and mounted on the bars, hundreds of bikes. Hundreds of bikes all looking the same. A soaked security guard is standing by the entrance to one of the compounds.

"Colour?" he says. "What colour are you?"

At another time and in another place it would have deserved a witty reply, but not today.

He gestures towards the row of different coloured flags at the entrance to each compound, all of which are bent almost horizontal by the wind.

"What colour group are you in?"

Memories of the registration desk are stirred and I fumble for the envelope inside my jacket pocket. The rain has got through, but helpfully there is a coloured flag printed on each piece of paper and although the ink has run, the colour remains. The man sees it and gestures in the direction of the compound with the green flag.

"Number?" he says.

"401," I say smugly. I'd been given my rider number a couple of weeks ago. He ticks his sodden list.

I find my bike but realise I have a problem. I've forgotten to bring the tools that I need to tighten the handlebars and fit the pedals. Two rows away somebody else is sorting out their bike and I can see that they've got a full set of tools. Alongside is an old but expensive looking bike travel box. The box is worn and covered with stickers of various types and sizes - bike components, travel information and bike events. This is no Sunday rider. I walk over, but they have their back to me.

"Excuse me," I say.

No response, my voice no match for the wind. I repeat myself, but still nothing and I touch their shoulder. They jerk forward, startled - disproportionately so.

"Jesus you made me jump." It's a woman's voice with an Irish twang.

She turns to face me. Her face is mostly concealed within the hood of her jacket, but her eyes are piercing blue and her expression accusatory.

"I'm sorry," I say, "I couldn't make myself heard above the wind."

I think about introducing myself, but something tells me that this is not going to be a long conversation.

" I've left my tools in my bag, could I borrow an Allen key and a pedal spanner?" I ask.

Without saying anything, she hands me a box of tools. I mumble thanks and go back to my bike.

I look over at the woman. Although I can't see clearly, her bike looks new and expensive. She's finished getting her bike ready and I hurry to sort mine out before going back to return the tools. I hand them to her and she nods. I feel I should make more conversation and notice a pair of wheels leaning up against her bike box.

"Nice wheels," I say and inwardly wince. Is that the best I can come up with? It feels like I've just said *'Nice tits'*.

She pulls a face. "Yes, but no good in this wind, I've had to put those on." She nods towards her bike.

I've no real understanding of what differentiates one pair of wheels from the another and decide to retreat. I probably strike her as a real biking numpty and there's no reason to open my mouth and confirm it. I wish her a good ride and go back to my bike.

Crouching down and pretending to make some final adjustments, I watch her pick up the spare wheels and walk out of the compound. I'm confused, surely she can't be taking the wheels with her. We're camping each night and limited to how much we can take. I'd had enough trouble packing the bare minimum, so how the hell can she carry a spare set of wheels?

Instead of walking in the direction of the main base camp, she turns towards the car park alongside the bike compound and ducks under the barrier. Through the gloom I see a flash of lights and the rear tailgate of a black 4x4 lifts. The woman puts the wheels in the boot before walking back to the main camp area. The car is parked up against the barrier and as soon as she is out of sight, I go over and have a look. I'm convinced that it's *the* 4x4. It's very Essex, tinted windows, garish alloy wheels, low profile tyres and led lights. Parking in a field is no doubt the nearest it's ever been to going off-road. Perched on the top of the dashboard is a thin lever arch file with a colourful cover. The pattern looks familiar. The rain begins to fall heavily so I abandon being nosy and start running towards the base camp.

The briefing is being held in what is euphemistically called the Chill Out Area. This is a large tented structure resembling a Bedouin tent with a sculptured roof and open sides. I'd settle for chilled, as no doubt would the five hundred or so people crammed inside. We're all frozen. The rain sprays horizontally through the open sides or collects in the scalloped roof before seeping through leaking seams. No Bedouin has ever encountered a howling south westerly like this.

Undaunted, the organisers stick to the script. Introductions are made to everyone. The Haskin bigwigs, the route organisers, the doctors, the security men, the physios, the caterers, the lorry drivers, the motorbike outriders... the list is endless. Nobody is forgotten which, under normal circumstances, would be commendable, but all I want to do is eat and go to sleep.

Half an hour later I really have had a enough of good causes and how the ride will bring out the very best in all of us. The 'Find Yourself. There's More There' mantra is repeated over and over again and is beginning to grate. I almost find myself getting up and ramming the microphone down their bloody do-gooder throats. If I don't eat soon, there will be *nothing* there. Just as it looks like it's coming to an end, it's the celebrity introductions - the elite riders who will inspire us to greater achievements. I can see Bob and Lawrence applauding loudly, no doubt Lawrence is wetting the padded inserts of his bib shorts.

Finally, we are introduced to the Trans-Global professional cycling team who are, we are told, using the ride as preparation for the Tour de France. There are ten riders, mostly Eastern European except for a couple of Italians and a British guy. I probably should have heard of them, but haven't. The team stand on the stage and wave and I'm convinced that Lawrence is having an orgasm. Their team colours are bright and the pattern distinctive. The same pattern which covered the lever arch file on the 4x4's dashboard.

Night....

I feel sick. I've moved from carb depletion to carb overload. The food tent was still busy when I finally got there; the caterers had certainly picked up on the need for white food, there was hardly a glimpse of anything red or resembling meat. After a full plate of ravioli and two bread rolls, I incorrectly decided that a plate of spaghetti followed by apple crumble and custard would be a good idea.

It then took me nearly half an hour to find my tent, of which twenty minutes were spent trudging around a mired field in the wind and the rain. The tents were in colour coded compounds, so no problem. I found the green compound and walked up and down the neat rows of numbered tents, but there was no sodding tent numbered 401. I decided to do what men find so difficult, I asked for help. Back to the main camp area only to be told that the tents were not numbered the same as your rider number and your tent number was written on the written information in the envelope. Bloody great!

The head light I'm wearing illuminates the depressing mess that is the inside of my tent. Not that you really need a light, despite the crap weather and it being past midnight, it's no darker than dusk. One bit of advice they'd given beforehand was to pack clothes and your sleeping bag in plastic bags. I'd dithered about whether to bother or not, but was now very pleased I had as at least something was dry. I've stripped off most of my soaked clothes and am sitting in my sleeping bag in damp pants. My immediate problem, forgetting chronic indigestion, is that I desperately need a pee. After consuming enough carbs, I'd begun worrying about water intake. I'd drunk less than a litre all day, so doubled that during dinner. It now feels like every last bit of that litre wants to burst out of my bladder in one go. I consider my options. I haven't washed or brushed my teeth, so I could get dressed and trek back to the main camp area to use the portable toilet cabins with basins and hot water, or I could forget about ablutions, get dressed and use one of the single toilet pods on the perimeter of the camping compound, or....

If anyone cared to look out of their tent, they'd be able to see me on my knees outside the tent wearing nothing but a pair of underpants and watch a steady and never ending stream of urine adding to the rivulets of rainwater running across the field. If they could hear above the roar of the wind, they could hear my groan of relief as my bladder gradually contracts.

Back in the tent and sleeping bag, I decide that I'm not fighting anymore and tomorrow will have to take care of itself. I'm going to sleep. Hopefully they'll be a couple of hours before the tent starts its journey to the Orkneys. I think about Mike and wonder where he is. With any luck he either got himself admitted and is being tended by a comely nurse who likes the Internet, or has booked himself into a comfy B&B in Wick.

One last thing. I pull out my phone from my jacket pocket and check it. There are no calls, but there are a number of messages of support and encouragement from friends and family, which somehow makes me feel warmer.

Something else has fallen out of the pocket. A blue packet - the moist wipes I'd bought at the airport. Christ, that feels like an age ago. Something written on the packet catches my eye, *alcohol free*. Maybe Bob bought the ones with alcohol which explains why he needed so many. If mine did contain alcohol, I'd rip open the packet and suck each one dry.

Day One

Morning....

'Bicycle, bicycle, bicycle - I want to ride my bicycle, bicycle, bicycle, bicycle - I want to ride my bike'. Why the hell is Freddie Mercury part of my dream? I'm on my bike being chased by a monster 4x4, my legs are spinning round, but the bike isn't moving and my head is full of his voice. I force myself awake to escape from the dream but the music doesn't stop. As my head clears, it slowly registers that the music is real and wasn't part of my subconscious state. It's coming from the public address system. I stare at my watch - five thirty. They'd told us at last night's briefing that we'd be woken up at five thirty; they hadn't said how or admitted to a twisted sense of humour.

The music stops and all I can hear is the sound of tents being unzipped; my head joins rows of others peering out at the new morning. How many of them are like me and questioning what the hell they're doing here? The gale appears to have blown itself out, the wind is lighter and it's stopped raining. I collapse back into the warmth of my sleeping bag and contemplate disappearing inside it; zipping it shut over my head, shutting my eyes and abandoning my future to fate.

It's ten to six and I'm in a field standing in a slow moving queue edging towards the green toilet cabin.

This is taking too long. I've still got to get my cycling gear on, pack my bag, eat breakfast, pick up my bike and get to the start line by seven o'clock. As the queue gets closer to the toilet I can see inside, there's an empty row of urinals - so why are we queuing? I realise that the queue is for the individual WC cubicles, the essential destination for those with well ordered body clocks. Mine is not well ordered, I only want a pee, a wash and to clean my teeth. Mumbling something to that effect I walk past the queue. The pee and wash are easy, but cleaning teeth is forbidden in the toilets for hygiene reasons. There is a sign asking that people use the separate teeth washing facilities.

The facilities turn out to be an open air plastic trough with eight taps connected to a cold water supply. I've always considered that brushing your teeth is a private affair, a bit like cutting your toenails or picking your nose, but I wait patiently in yet another queue. Eight people in front of me, brush, swoosh, gargle and spit, the sounds all mingling together into one confused mixture of noise. How much better it would be if there was some form of co-ordination.

Sweat is dripping off my face and down my neck and I haven't turned a pedal yet. Somehow

I've made it to the start, not quite on time, but not that it matters as nothing is moving. About fifty yards ahead is the start line bouncy castle and splaying out from it there is a sea of cyclists patiently waiting to start. At the front speeches are being made about personal endeavour and self sacrifice. As soon as they're finished, the VIP's making the speeches will no doubt get in their cars or catch a plane to make the journey home. Nine days later they'll get to Land's End the same way and use the same platitudes to welcome us.

Occasionally someone pushes or barges their way past me. It reminds me of a ski lift queue, when someone, usually a pubescent German youth, decides that they have a God given right to sod everyone else and get to the front.

My leaving preparations were far from ordered. Packing rapidly became stuffing, with me finally sitting on my bag so the zip would fasten. Breakfast was quick, very quick. By the time I'd lugged my bag to the lorry which would take it to tonight's base camp, run to the bike compound, picked up my bike and got to the start, I was knackered.

I'd looked for the black 4x4, but it had gone. I looked for the girl and her bike, but they'd gone too.

Bagpipes! It was inevitable that there would be bagpipes and of course they are playing Scotland the Brave. As the drone drifts across with the wind, I sense movement and the mass of riders and bikes gradually edge forward. Ten minutes later I ride over the start line, people clap, take photographs and wish us luck. It's a nice feeling.

We start going the wrong way and head north. The pipers have led us down into the centre of John O'Groats and have stopped in the middle of the road, playing on as we ride around them and return back the way we've come. I take in the ambience of John O'Groats - Christ what a dump! It's a car park with a cafe, gift shop and a derelict gothic hotel. I don't waste my time looking for the famous sign pointing to Land's End. I'd overheard that it belongs to the man who has the concession for taking photographs in front of it and because so many signs have been stolen as souvenirs, he unbolts it and takes it home each night. It's a cynicism that seems to afflict both John O'Groats and Land's End. I've been to Land's End once and from what I can remember, in terms of ugliness there's little to chose between them; their only claim to fame being the geographical fact that they are situated at the extremes of the British mainland. It strikes me as perverse that people expend so much effort and energy in getting from one to the other.

We're riding one hundred and four miles today, with stops at thirty five and seventy five miles. Mentally I need to break it down into three separate rides as my training involved only one ride over a hundred miles and that was tough.

For the first ten or so miles we ride inland in a westerly direction, the roads are reasonably flat, the scenery bleak and unspectacular. A few miles before Thurso we get close to the sea and the wind picks up, blowing across the road which unsettles the bike a bit, but I'm grateful that it's not a headwind. The road dips down into Thurso and back up out. The town is still asleep and I wonder just how awake it is when it's awake. I get up off the saddle and sit down again, wriggling to get comfortable. *Shit!* I forgot to put chamois cream on and have left it my bag. It's a bit daft calling it chamois cream, it's been some time since cycling shorts used chamois leather to protect one's vitals. However, even with today's high tech fabrics, it still requires the application of copious amounts of lubricating cream to avoid your most tender skin being ravaged and ripped apart. I think about asking someone at the first pit stop if they've got some cream I can use, but decide it's one of those things you just don't share, like a toothbrush, KY jelly, or a face flannel.

Riding with a group in single file along a narrow road, I hear a shout from back of the line. For some reason serious cyclists do a lot of shouting and I haven't yet been able to make out what it's all about. This time it has a more agitated tone to it. About ten cyclists ride pass at high speed and I recognise the Trans-Global pattern on the back of their jerseys. Shit they're fast! I had no idea just how fast professional cyclists were. Not far behind are the men and women elite riders, all wearing the same Haskin Long Britain Ride clothing.

About ten minutes later there is another shout and a group of about twenty riders ride past. They are mainly men, but there are a couple of women. They're not quite as fast as the others that have gone past, but they're still bloody quick. I recognise the slight figure of Lawrence towards the front and then a girl with blond hair tied in a pony tail goes past. She seems familiar, or at least her bike does. The jigsaw is slowly fitting slowly together, Irish, blue eyes and blond hair. I notice a scorpion on her bum. The scorpion, a manufacturer's logo appears to be smiling.

Flags by the side of the road signal the first pit stop and it's a welcome sight. A marshall stands in the middle of the road gesturing riders to slow down and turn into the car park of a village hall. The car park is packed with cyclists and bikes and there is a queue for everything; to get food, to refill your water bottle, to go to the toilet...queuing is becoming a big part of my life.

I have food first and crouch down on a grass verge with a cream cheese and onion fajita wrap, a pork pie, a packet of prawn cocktail crisps and a banana. Under normal circumstances, a pretty unpalatable mixture, but today delicious. The next thing is to go to the toilet. They are inside the hall with the queue spilling out of the front door and a suitable tree a couple of miles down the road strikes me as a far better idea.

There's a rubbing sensation between my legs, it's not painful - well at least not yet. A medic estate car is parked in the car park with the tailgate lifted and a line of people waiting in a queue. A woman wearing a sweatshirt with *MEDIC* written across it is standing nearby and I ask if they've got some chamois cream. She smiles benignly and points to the queue - it seems I'm not alone. The rider at the front of the queue goes up to a man dressed in a green tunic, they have a brief chat before the rider slips off the straps of his bib shorts and turns his back. The man puts on a pair of blue rubber gloves, dips his hand in a tub of cream, pulls down the man's shorts. exposing a white bottom and proceeds to apply the cream liberally and vigorously. I flex my legs and shuffle - hardly any discomfort at all. I walk back towards my bike.

A man smiles at me, an older man with a big plaster over his chin.

Guilt! I'd totally forgotten about Mike.

I'm really pleased to see him, we shake hands and he tells me his story. A nurse at the hospital had taken him under her wing. He admitted to no more than that. Her son is a taxi driver and was taking people from Wick Airport to the base camp, so she arranged for him to pick up Mike's bag. She had a spare room so put Mike up for the night and cooked him dinner. In the morning, she'd made breakfast and then the son had driven Mike to the camp for the start. The organisers wanting to look after their oldest entrant, had got his bike ready and he'd jumped out of the taxi and straight onto his bike. They'd put him at the front for the start and he's made the first thirty five miles without any problems. I'm convinced that Mike could fall into the proverbial and come up smelling of roses.

"This is Gillian," Mike says and turns towards the woman standing next to him.

Whilst Mike was telling his story, I'd tried my best to avoid looking at her, but struggled. Probably around forty, her face is pleasant and she strikes me as the quintessential English mum. If I was younger and looking for a new mum, she'd fit the bill perfectly. Apart from her chest that is. Organ stops are the only way to describe her nipples which stick out from her cycling jersey like... well organ stops. Presumably she must know, surely they can be concealed by a decent bra or a couple of strategically placed Elastoplasts.

Gillian smiles and holds out her hand. I force myself to look her in the eye.

"Gillian and I are going to ride together. We seem to go at the same pace," Mike says.

I give him the benefit of the doubt and accept that his motives are confined to cycling. Something jogs my memory.

"Do you remember Lawrence, he was on the coach? Did you see him stop with a number of quick riders?"

"Sorry the coach journey is a bit of a blur. There was a fast group, but they didn't stop long," Mike answers.

"You didn't notice a blond girl did you?

Mike shakes his head, uninterested in the question. I consider telling him about the 4x4 and the girl, but decide he's probably not interested. It's not such an ill wind that blew him into the comforting arms of a nurse with a spare room and a woman with organ stop nipples.

Five miles after the pit stop we hit the first big hills. At first we skirt the coast and then turn inland and the scenery changes to how I think Scotland should look. Undulating roads surrounded by bare rock and soaring sheer cliffs. I grind my way on, getting more and more pissed off as people pass me on the uphill stretches, but resisting the temptation to try and keep up with them. The only way I can hope to finish this ride is to keep to my own pace.

I start thinking about the girl and the 4x4 again. Why the hell am I so obsessed? It's probably because I haven't got much else to think about and it takes my mind off the next eight days. I haven't really spoken to anybody apart from Mike; lots of acknowledging nods, a few good mornings, but no real conversations. Since the briefing I haven't seen Bob or Lawrence, no doubt they've already finished today's stage and gone for a quick run. Nobody actually seems over friendly, but there again, I haven't really wanted to speak to people either. Perhaps following the baptism by the elements at John O'Groats, we're all a bit nervous and subdued.

Afternoon....

The compass on my bike computer changes from west to south - finally we're heading in the right direction. We turn at Bettyhill where, after a torturous climb into the village, there is a wonderful view of the sands, cliffs and sea at Torrisdale Bay. Heading out of Bettyhill, the climbing is over, it's true! Going south *is* downhill.

Although the road which runs alongside the River Naver is flowing and gently undulating, by the time it leaves the forest and the land opens up around Loch Naver, I'm beginning to feel tired. There's forty miles between the first and second pit stops and the first twenty of hard climbing is beginning to have an effect. At the end of the loch the road dips down over a bridge and beyond that I can see the welcome sight of the second pit stop in a pub car park. It's a place called Altnaharra but as far as I can see, the pub is the only vestige of civilisation.

As I queue for food, large groups of cyclists are leaving and I fear that I'm one of the last, but the steady stream of cyclists on the other side of the loch heading toward the stop, allay my fears. I can't help but overhear the depressing news that there's a long climb soon after we leave the stop.

My bike computer shows that there are only about three miles to the finish and my legs find a little bit more energy from somewhere. The climb after the stop wasn't as bad as predicted, long, but not too steep. The twenty miles since has been a glorious downhill roll through to the town of Lairg before following Achany Glen to the edge of the Kyle of Sutherland.

Two hundred yards ahead a motorcycle outrider is waving traffic on the opposite of the road to slow down; he waves his other hand beckoning me to turn right. Twenty feet across bumpy ground and then the smooth matting of the finish bouncy castle. A hooter blows, a small group clap and say well done. The first day's ride is over and it feels good.

I get off my bike as stiff as hell and the ground moves in the same way it does when you get off a boat after a long time at sea. The bike compound is not far away and as I walk towards it, I thank my bike for performing faultlessly and apologise that it's going to be left out in the cold again. It doesn't answer, but our relationship is one of comfortable silence.

I'm putting the bike up on the rail and notice a man striding towards me. He doesn't strike me as a rider. Mid-forties, he's wearing corduroy trousers, a sports jacket and brogue shoes, his face is heavily tanned and his blond hair is swept back over his forehead. Expecting him to say something, I look towards him, but he brushes past before ducking under the barrier into the car park. Walking at right angles to him is a woman with blond hair and they meet at a black 4x4. I can hear a raised male voice and see him gesticulating with his hands. The woman shouts back at him, but slowly her body hunches up and she edges away from him. Suddenly, she turns and half walks, half runs away. He gets into the car and drives out, wheels spinning and throwing clods of mud into the air.

I'm surprised to find the inside of my tent welcoming, but somehow it is. It's absorbed some heat out of the little sun there's been and is a refuge from the chill wind. My bag is still outside. Luckily the green tent compound isn't too far away from where the bags have been left in an ordered colour coded pile. There were quite a few to be collected by people still riding which made me feel a bit smug. Across the field there's a long queue for the *Posh Wash* showers, the cabins differentiated from the toilet by being painted blue instead of green. From the back pocket of my jersey I retrieve a long packet containing a salami stick and a chocolate fudge bar which I'd picked up at the second stop. Never before had such mundane food looked so appetising.

Suddenly I'm thirsty and crave a cup of tea. The shower queue hasn't gone down, so I drag my bag into the tent, pull out my jacket which is still damp and head towards the catering tent. It's practically deserted except for a few people taking advantage of the flat floor and stretching to loosen tight muscles. It's something that I should be doing, but I haven't got the energy.

I dunk the tea bag in the tepid water which dribbles out of a massive urn. Tiny brown specs float to the top and form a film over the surface as milk is added. At least it's warm and wet as they say. Most people are sitting alone which is something I can understand. The blond woman is sitting by herself at the far end of the tent.

"Can I join you?" I ask.

Like our first conversation, she doesn't appear to hear me. She doesn't look up as I sit down and stares into her polystyrene cup as she gently stirs the contents with a wooden stick.

"How did you find the ride today?"

She looks up, her blue eyes greyer and red around the edges - she's been crying. I've become an expert in knowing when women have been crying. For the first time I see her face properly. Her skin is pale and porcelain-like, although her cheeks glow red, no doubt due to the effort of a day's cycling. She's not wearing any make-up and her shoulder length light blond hair has subtle strawberry highlights.

"Sorry, did you say something? I was miles away," she says and looks around her. No doubt questioning why I should pick this table to sit at with so many empty places.

"How did you find the ride today?" I repeat.

"Tough."

"What time did you finish?" I ask.

"Around one o'clock."

"Christ, that's impressive."

"Not really."

"We've met before," I say, "at John O'Groats, you lent me some tools."

She seems to relax a bit. Looking up from the cup, she asks, "And what about you, how did you do?"

"Okay, but this cycling is all new to me. Steady Eddie that's me, I just want to finish."

She half smiles. "Don't we all."

"I'm Mark," I hold out my hand.

She takes it, her grip light and warm. "Sinead."

"As in...." Prat! How many people must say that to her?

She interrupts. "Yes, as in O'Connor, but in my case really as in O'Connor. I can't blame my parents, nobody had heard of the other Sinead O'Connor when I was born."

"Pity I can't say the same about my parents."

"Why?" she says. "What's your surname?

"Anthony."

It takes a little time for it to register, as it does with most people.

"Mark Anthony as in...."

It's my turn to interrupt. "As in Antony and Cleopatra - yes. The only difference is that I have an 'h' in my name, not that it makes a blind bit of difference. At least with your name you can get a restaurant booking. Nobody ever believes a Roman general is coming to eat.

She looks as if she's trying to resist, but laughs and her eyes become bright blue again.

Someone calls out her name loudly. The man from the 4x4 is standing by the door and Sinead stops laughing.

"I've got to go...it's my husband."

Evening....

Where the hell does the time go to? It's a quarter to eight and I haven't started to sort out and repack the contents of my bag which I've emptied out over the floor of the tent. The *Posh Wash* showers confounded my expectations. Once I'd endured the cold wait outside, they are great, clean with loads of hot water. There was only one bit that didn't feel good, the sting when the soap touched my tender patches. I can't afford to forget the cream again.

There's a compulsory briefing at eight o'clock in the chill-out area. The chill-out area isn't in a Bedouin tent today, instead it's in a tent which resembles a large Indian tepee. Obviously the weather on the prairie is worse than the desert and the tent has sides and a sensible roof.

The briefing has been delayed by fifteen minutes and I have an idea. I go to the information desk and ask if they can give me the rider number of Sinead O'Connor. I make up a story that she's a friend of a friend and I would like to say hello to her. Her name doesn't spark any sign of recognition with the girl behind the desk, she's clearly too young to have heard of Sinead O'Connor. Armed with this information, I go to the desk which allocates tent numbers as people arrive back and ask if they could let me have the tent number for rider No 345, explaining that I have borrowed some tools from them and need to give them back. Her tent number is No 1 in the green compound which probably means that she was the first rider back amongst the green group. Her tent is a long way from mine.

I walk past where they are giving massages and physio. Inevitably there's a long queue of people waiting. Through the open flap of the tent I can see four rows of five tables and on each table someone is being pummeled, pushed and pulled by young children. They're not really young children, they just look it. I'd read that they are student physios who are giving their time for free in order to gain experience. Men and women lie alongside one another in various states of undress - it's no place for a wilting violet.

Mike is waiting in the queue and I make a weak joke, advising him not to offer money for something extra. He barely laughs, he looks tired and fed up and the plaster over his chin is looking dirty.

"I've been waiting for over an hour. It's not fair. If you're one of the fit quick riders and get back early, you go straight in, but us slower ones who actually need some help have to wait. By the time I get to eat they'll have eaten all the best food and I'll be left with the stuff no one wants."

He has a point, it doesn't seem right. I tell him that I haven't eaten yet to try and make him feel better, but it doesn't seem to improve his mood.

The briefing is mercifully short and to the point. A quick run through of tomorrow's route, a mere ninety nine miles down to Fort William via the shores of Loch Ness with one stinker of a climb shortly after the start and another halfway in. The weather forecast is cloudy with rain later in the day.

I'm aware of somebody trying to catch my attention as I'm about to sit down for dinner, a woman I don't recognise at first, but then realise that it's Gillian, the woman with organ stop nipples. She's wearing a fleece top and I wonder if it's specially reinforced as there is no discernable evidence of any bodily protuberances. We chat and she's very pleasant. She's married with three kids and her husband rowed the Atlantic last year, so she decided to do the ride to prove that she was also capable of doing something remarkable. She also wanted to get her own back for all the months he'd left her alone with three children. She's been a runner for years and has moved on to triathlons so she was fairly fit before. I tell her about my divorce and she's sympathetic. I'm not sure I hear her right, but think she says something like my wife must have been mad to let me go. It hasn't happened for a long time, but I think she's flirting with me. I smile and she smiles back. She's wearing make-up and I concede that she's not an unattractive woman, but not really my type. It's difficult to fancy someone you think would make a good surrogate mother.

Night....

A detour on the way back to my tent after dinner brings me to end of the tent compound where the tent numbering starts. Although it's ten o'clock, it's still light and I can see No 1, but don't want to get too close. Anyway the flap is securely zipped up and there's no sign of life.

It's half past eleven and I've finally made some sense of the contents of my bag. I've laid out what's needed for tomorrow morning and packed the rest of the stuff away reasonably tidily. I need to go to the toilet in order to prevent having to get up in the middle of the night, but there are too many people about to repeat last night's performance. Coincidently I use the farthest toilet pod which takes me past tent No 1.

There's a dull light inside and the sides of the tent bulge as the person inside moves around. At least I assume it's one person. If two people were sharing it would be a bloody tight fit. I picture her husband in his sports jacket and corduroy trousers and decide that he's not the camping sort. Sinead must be sleeping alone.

Despite being dog tired I'm wide awake. I don't want to look at my watch to see what time it is as it would be too depressing. In the quiet of the night it's amazing how sound travels between the tents; each rustle of a sleeping bag, each cough, the resonance of snoring and the breaking of wind, all conspire to keep me awake. Waiting for sleep, I question again why it is that I'm so hung up on this girl called Sinead. I put together everything I know and make up a rational scenario. She's a very good cyclist, but he's not and has come along to support her. He doesn't like camping, so he's staying in local hotels or guest houses. Okay, he's not a good driver, but that applies to the majority of 4x4 drivers. The row? All couples row, there's nothing unusual about that. So what's my problem?

The last thing I remember before finally falling asleep is a loud fart, it sounds pretty close - perhaps it was me.

Day Two

Morning....

As I jump the queue, I'm grateful that my body clock is still on a different setting to the ten or so people waiting patiently for the WC cubicles. The person responsible for the early morning wake up music has not lost their sense of humour and *Ride of the Valkyries* is still ringing in my ears. I'm already in my cycling gear and trying hard to ignore the disconcerting feeling of my buttocks slipping and sliding together. Maybe I've overdone the cream, but it's better to be safe than sorry.

A layer of low morning mist is backlit by the rising sun and creates silhouettes of people as they move silently around the sea of tents. It really looks quite eerie and surreal. It's not raining but the heavy dew has soaked the long grass and I can feel the dampness seeping through my trainers. I'm getting used to dampness.

Last night's preparation makes final packing fairly simple and my bag zips up without having to sit on it. I drop the bag off at the lorry and head towards the food tent for breakfast carrying my cycling gear. There's still forty five minutes before the start and I congratulate myself on my new-found organisational skills.

The food tent is heaving with people, but the caterers are efficient and it's not long before I've got my bowl of porridge with honey, a couple of slices of toast and a banana. Mike is sitting at a table on the other side of the tent and I catch his eye. He waves and smiles and seems happier than last night. I look but can't see Sinead.

So much for my organisational skills! I'm in the bike compound staring at my feet. I'm wearing wet trainers and carrying my cycling shoes. Unfortunately I only have one pair of feet and my trainers should be in my bag, which is in the lorry. I could walk back and politely ask the big guys who stow the bags if they would kindly unload the lorry until they find my bag. Then I could put my trainers in my bag, give it back to the big guys and ask them to re-load the lorry. I could do all of that, but dismiss it as a very stupid idea. The trainers won't go in my jersey pockets, so I tie the laces together and hang them around my neck, but realise that when I'm riding they'll dangle down and irritate the hell out of me. So I unzip my jersey and tuck them inside, luckily the jersey material stretches just enough. It also looks ridiculous and I decide to carry the trainers until just after the start, then I'll stop and stuff them into my jersey.

I walk with the bike and join the starting queue. Although I'm earlier than yesterday, I'm not much nearer the start line. The slower riders should start first, with the quicker ones behind and the elite riders starting last. However, it seems that almost all riders want to get off as early as possible in one big mass. People are walking past me as they make their way to the back of the queue. I recognise Sinead and look straight at her, but she looks through me. I'm wearing my helmet and console myself that I'm lost in a montage of helmets, bikes and Lycra. Had she realised that she was looking for the only cyclist with a pair of trainers round his neck, I'm sure she would have recognised me immediately.

She's chatting to someone next to her and smiling, her eyes sparkling again. Her replica team jersey hugs her slim body and the back view is just as pleasing. The scorpion on her bum is still smiling. Lucky bugger. If I'm ever reincarnated I want to come back into this world as a Lycra scorpion.

After about five miles of riding on easy main roads, the route turns right onto a 'B' road and immediately starts to climb sharply. I'm struggling. My legs are hardly warmed up and more and more people ride past. Mercifully the road levels off a bit as it sweeps around a wide bend and I manage to get a bit of breath back. After the bend there is a less steep but long ascent and I drag myself up. At the top, cars are parked by the side of the road and people cheer us on. Quite a few riders stop to recover, but as much as I'm tempted to stop, I carry on, seeing it as my chance to regain some places. No matter how many times I tell myself that this isn't a race, I can't help feeling bad when somebody passes me and good when I manage to overtake.

The road doesn't immediately descend and is fairly level for a mile or so. A group of riders pass me going very quickly. At first I assume that it's the Trans-Global team or one of the elite rider groups, but realise that they're not all wearing the same kit. They are one of the fast club groups and I recognise Lawrence and then Sinead riding a few places behind him.

The descent is spoilt by a pot holed and rutted road surface which requires a lot of concentration; the handlebars feel like a jack hammer as each imperfection is the road is transmitted into my arms. A couple of riders have suffered punctures, which is not surprising with this road surface. I've learnt that you don't stop to help people with punctures; you might shout and ask if they are alright, but then you ride past before they have the chance to answer. Anybody with real problems will be sorted out by the mobile mechanic vans.

A third person has stopped with a puncture, but this time I pull my brakes on with all the strength I can muster. The back wheel is off Sinead's bike and an inner tube has been discarded by the side of the road.

"Hi, are you all right - can I help?" I ask.

She's obviously put in a new tube and is now trying to get the tyre back on the rim, but is struggling.

Without looking up she replies, "No I'm fine - just fine."

I assume that she hasn't recognised me and take off my helmet. "Sinead, it's me Mark.

 Can I do anything?"

She throws the wheel and tyre at me. "Yes, get the sodding tyre on." Tears of frustration are rolling down her cheeks.

 There is the last six inches of the tyre to go back on the rim and I push the tyre as hard as I can. I desperately want it to slip easily into place so I can achieve hero status, but the rubber is so tight it won't go over. There are some tyre levers on the ground and I pick them up,

"Don't use them, you'll pinch the tube," she snaps.

"I don't think there's any choice, I can't push the tyre over."

I hesitate. She's right, there's a very real risk that I'll pinch and puncture the new tube, but I can't see any alternative. As gently as I can, I insert one lever under the rim and prise the tyre over. It suddenly slips into place, but I've no idea whether I've nicked the tube with the tyre lever or not.

"Have you got a pump?" I ask.

She snatches the wheel back and pulls a CO2 canister out of her saddlebag. I hold my breath as the canister releases the CO_2 into the tyre. We both feel the tyre. It's hard and appears to be staying that way.

I've never seen a rear wheel go back on a bike so quickly and without saying a word, Sinead gets on the bike and rides off. I pick up the discarded tube and tyre levers and put them in my jersey pocket.

Five miles before the first stop I'm overtaken by a group of male elite riders who are followed a little later by the women's group. There's been no sign of the Trans-Global team which strikes me as a bit odd.

At the first stop there's a girl sitting at a table and staring at a laptop which is monitoring the timing equipment as each rider crosses the line. I open a conversation by saying that her job looks pretty boring and she agrees. I get her to explain how it all works and ask about rider No 345. I say we're members of the same club and that I'm interested to know how good she is.

The girl scrolls through the screen.

"O'Connor, well she's been through already. Looking at the times she was with a group of good riders, probably top club riders," she answers.

"They went past me today and they looked almost as fast as the elite riders."

"Well there are a lot of very good amateurs and ex-pro riders taking part.

"So she's pretty good then? Well for a girlie?"

She laughs.

I'm conscious that I'm asking a lot of questions, but have one more and hope my charm lasts.

"What's happened to the Trans-Global team, have they been overawed by the little old ladies with baskets on the front of their bikes?"

She laughs again. "There certainly is a mixture of riders. No, Trans-Global have decided to start much later, something about wanting to ride at the same time of day as professional events."

I thank her, grab something to eat and get back on the bike.

Now this really feels like Scotland - Loch Ness. I remember the route from the briefing last night and know that we are going to ride practically the whole length of the western shore.

However, the ride is tough and disappointing. Tough because the road undulates steeply, disappointing because you don't see a lot of the loch The road runs slightly away from the loch and there is an almost constant curtain of trees which hides any views of the water. However, at one point the road gets close to the loch and there's a wooden boat jetty and a small pebbly beach. On the jetty, four or five naked lads are running towards the loch. Seconds later I hear a splash and screams as they hit the water.

The road continues to rise and fall until it reaches the southern end of the loch where we climb into Fort Augustus and the second pit stop.

The person behind the timing computer is a burly guy with a big black beard, who's unlikely to succumb to my charm. I don't chance my luck again and join the queue for food. A group of women in front of me are talking and giggling about the skinny dippers. One of them comments in a loud voice that she didn't see anything that impressed her and the women dissolve into more giggles. The man in front of them turns and reminds them that the water would have been very cold. His tone is not altogether light hearted and a number of men in the queue including me, murmur in agreement. It's as he's defending a sexist attack - *young lady, we can't all be hung like a donkey and cold water does have a shrinking effect.* Can you imagine the female indignation if a group of men openly ridiculed a group of naked women for not being their idea of sexual perfection?

A voice is calling my name. A voice that everyone within a twenty yard radius can hear.

"Doing okay?" Bob shouts.

I'm suspicious of his friendliness. "Yes, not too bad Bob. You're not riding with Lawrence then?" I reply.

" No, I decided to let him have his head."

'Decided to let him have his head'. Why can't he just say that Lawrence is far too quick for him, instead of making it sound like he bestowed some gift upon him.

I realise why Bob is so friendly. He's run out of friends and he's somebody who must have people around him.

A woman rider who has just ridden in to the pit stop comes over to us. She starts to take off her helmet, but there's no need, one look at her chest and I know it's Gillian. We exchange pleasantries and I introduce her to Bob, who shakes her hand whilst staring at her nipples.

"You haven't been riding with Mike today then?" I say to Gillian.

"Well we started together, but he really struggled with the first big hill and by the time we got to the first stop he'd almost had it. He managed to start again, but after a couple of miles he decided to wait for the broom wagon."

The broom wagon is the coach which follows the route behind the riders and picks up anybody who's been forced to stop.

"That's a shame," I say, "he did so well yesterday."

Gillian pulls a face. "Not really, he only got as far as Bettyhill."

I'm surprised. "He didn't say anything," I say. "He told me that he'd got in late."

"He was late because he had to stay on the coach until they'd picked up all the stragglers from the last stage," Gillian replies. "He asked me not to say anything."

Her tone changes. "I'm worried about him. There's no way he's going to make it, but he's so bloody stubborn, he'll kill himself before he admits defeat."

Like it or not, Mike has become my problem. Well not so much a problem, more a responsibility. Gillian and I know that we've got to do something.

Bob continues to stare at Gillian's chest.

Afternoon....

I ride the last stage in a group of three, myself, Bob and Gillian. Most of the time I'm riding in single file because whenever he can, Bob rides alongside Gillian. I try to ride ahead, worried that Bob is not keeping his eyes on the road and will crash in front me. On the occasions that I ride alongside Gillian, Bob forces his front wheel between us and gradually pushes me out towards the oncoming traffic until I admit defeat and either accelerate forward or drop back.

The pace is reasonable and Bob and I seem to ride at roughly the same speed, despite his flash cycling club jersey. I've noticed that when I get tired I become grumpy and begin to pick holes in anything or anybody in close proximity. Bob is easy pickings. He's probably early to mid forties, but looks older because of his grey hair and old fashioned parting and fringe hairstyle which he's probably had all his life. Not that looking old would ever be a problem to him. I suspect he's always wanted to look older than he is and no doubt grew a soft down moustache as soon as he could. He'll be a big noise, both literally and figuratively, in his local Round Table and Golf Club and hold various committee memberships. His house will be in pretty village and he'll have his own seat in the saloon bar of the village pub where he'll drink noisily with his drinking chums who will all be clones of him. His wife.....I need to stop, my imagination is running away with me.

We follow the Caledonian Canal, then cycle past Loch Lochy, along the River Lochy and finally into the outskirts of Fort William. As we turn into the base camp, I feel good. Two days down and everything is still functioning, even my bum appears to be holding up. I've hardly noticed the pair of trainers strung around my neck and realise that Bob and Gillian haven't said anything about the two large projections sticking out from my collar bones, perhaps they thought it was some kind of deformity and were too polite to mention it.

I'm already slipping into some kind of a routine. I dump my bag in the tent, have a quick snack of whatever's left over from the second pit stop and then walk over to the food tent for a lukewarm cup of tea with a brown skin on it.

I'm lost in my thoughts when someone sits down next to me.

"I think I owe you an apology," Sinead says.

"That's alright, cycling's pretty stressful," I say, although I have no idea why she got herself into such a state over a puncture.

There's a pause and I sense that she's struggling to think of an explanation.

She breaks the silence. "What did you have under you jersey? It looked like a pair of shoes."

"It was," I answer.

"Why were you riding with a pair of shoes stuffed down your top?"

"I don't know really, it's just something I do. I've kind of got used to it."

I keep a straight face, but then smile and explain about the trainers. When I finish, I decide to ask her some questions. "Who were you riding with today?"

"Some club riders I met," she replies.

"You're very quick. You've obviously done a lot of cycling at a high level. "

She looks at me and gives me a resigned smile as if to say, *Okay you're not going to rest until you find out more.*

"I was good, but that was quite a few years ago. Since then I've only done club and regional events."

"So why do this ride?" I ask. "I can see why the elite guys do it, for the publicity and to keep their sponsors happy by riding for worthy causes, but what do you get out of it? What does your husband get out of it?"

Her body language changes and I know that I've ridden my luck.

Before she has a chance to answer and exactly on cue, the man in the sports jacket and corduroy trousers comes up and stands behind Sinead.

"I thought I might find you in here," he says. His voice isn't Irish, more middle England with a hint of manufactured poshness.

Sinead seems embarrassed. "Mark, this is Richard... my husband. Richard, this is Mark, he helped me with a puncture today."

Richard shakes my hand. Richard nearly breaks my fingers. It's as if he's marking his territory. His smile is false. "Nice to meet you Mark, thanks for helping Sinead. Now my dear, we really must go."

Sinead gets up and without looking at me, follows her husband out of the tent.

Gillian is in the queue for the Posh Wash showers and we talk about Mike. We agree that one of us needs to talk to him. Gillian thinks it would be best if it were me, her logic being that Mike may not take easily to a woman giving him advice. I think about his divorced wife and reluctantly agree. The broom wagon hasn't got back yet and I give Gillian my mobile number so she can ring me when she sees Mike.

We've reached the front of the queue and keep our eyes glued to the row of blue doors, mentally guessing which will open and be vacated first. Two doors open simultaneously and two glowing pink riders come down the steps. Gillian and I move forward, but are stopped by the attendant. This is a well ordered routine and two other attendants move forward with squeegee mops and sluice out torrents of waters from the floor of each cubicle. As good as they are, Posh Wash showers have a serious drainage problem.

The shower is amazing. I'm beginning to get the utmost pleasure from the simplest and most ordinary things. Normally a shower is, well just a shower, but now it is one of the most sensuous and exhilarating experiences a man can have. A chocolate fudge bar and a salami stick which under normal circumstances I ever eat, have become the two greatest foods available to man.

As I walk back to my tent, Bob passes me.

"Gillian," he says.

I've learnt that you need to insert a question mark after Bob's single words to make any sense of what he's saying. I tell him that the last time I saw her was in the shower queue and he heads off in that direction as if on a mission. I fear that Gillian might have a long seven days ahead of her. Even if she overcomes the cycling, she may have more problems overcoming the advances of Bob.

Evening....

Bloody hell - mountains! I look up and see mountains, well Ben Nevis to be more precise. Ben Nevis is towering over the campsite and the early evening sun is reflecting off its slopes. I've been so obsessed with looking for things on the ground - tents, toilets, showers, food tents...that I've not looked upwards. I make a mental note to look up more, otherwise I'm in danger of travelling the length of the country looking no further than a few feet in front of me.

Night....

I lie in my sleeping bag and look at my watch. It's half past ten and I haven't spoken to Mike. I saw Gillian across the food tent at dinner and she shook her head, indicating that she hadn't seen him. It's now raining and the sound is amplified by the tent fabric. I'm not looking forward to my trip across the field to the toilet pod, but at least I can go to the nearest one. I'd thought about trying to find out Sinead's tent number again, but decided there was no point. Whatever is going on in her world, she isn't going to let me in on it.

My mobile rings - Shit! Gillian tells me that Mike is in the food tent having a cup of coffee.

The tent is deserted, except for a Mike and a few bike mechanics and physios having a late dinner. He's hunched up, his hands cradling a cup of coffee as if trying to extract some comfort from the warmth. I take my wet jacket off and sit down opposite him. He doesn't seem surprised to see me.

"You as well?" he says.

"What do you mean?"

"Let me guess, you're going to tell me that I should give up and go home to my rocking chair and cup of Horlicks. Well that's what the organisers want. It would be bad form if one of their riders drops dead on them. It's what Gillian thinks, although she won't come out and say it."

"Okay Mike," I say, "I think you should give up and admit that you've bitten off more than you can chew. It's as simple as that. It's not the end of the world, go and book another holiday, go and seduce your nurse in Wick. Mike, you're not going to finish this ride and if you kill yourself trying, there'll be no more holidays and your nurse will find someone else."

Mike replies. "It seems that I don't have much choice. The small print says three broom wagons and you're out. If I don't finish tomorrow, it's over anyway, so I've nothing to lose by giving it another try."

"Do you know what tomorrow's rides is like? It's one hundred and fifteen miles. Over Glen Coe first thing with fifty miles before the first pit stop."

A look of resignation comes over Mike's face and then he chuckles. "They're pretty amazing aren't they? I'll miss them."

There's no need for him to explain what he's talking about. "Yes well they're probably the best memory you'll have of all this."

He digs in his pocket and hands me a business card. "My address is on there, if you're ever in

Ilfracombe, pop in for a cup of tea or I'll do you a deal on a room for the night."

I take the card and stand up. Mike stands up and we shake hands, then we hug. I'm surprised, I don't do man hugs.

Walking back to the tent, the place is deserted except for the security guys at the bike compound, their day-glo jackets illuminated by the compound's arc lights. The only other light is coming from one of the Trans-Global motorhomes parked in the car park. The light gets brighter as the front door opens and a man and woman leave the coach. The man gets into a black 4x4 and drives away. The woman walks towards the tent compound.

I know I should go straight to my tent, get into my sleeping bag and forget what I've seen. Instead I walk towards Sinead.

 When she's about twenty feet away, I stop and wait for her. Her head is dipped, but as she passes she looks up.

"What the hell are you doing here?" she asks. I don't get the impression that she's pleased to see me.

"I was walking back to my tent and I saw you."

"So?"

"So, I just wanted to make sure you were alright."

"And why the hell shouldn't I be alright?"

It's a question that I struggle to answer, because I don't know the answer myself. I try to be honest. "Because....because you don't seem happy, something went wrong with your ride on the first day and today your reaction to the puncture....." I run out of words.

I can see that she's carefully thinking about her reply. "Okay, you're right. Richard and I are having a few problems and we thought that if he came on the ride to support me, it would help, but it hasn't. So that's why I'm upset at times.....and you're not really helping, he can be a little possessive."

"I'm sorry, I guess I should mind my own business," I say, although I don't mean it.

She touches my arm. "No, it's me who should be sorry. I'm being a bit of cow and you're being so sweet."

Sweet, that'll do for tonight.

"Okay," I say, "I'll butt out and leave you alone."

"I think that would be best," she says, before turning and walking away.

Day Three

Morning....

It's no good, like it or not and as unexpected as it is, I've got to admit that it's the same feeling I had when I met *her* for the first time at Le Mans.

It took me by surprise then. The team had finally accepted that the engine of the car was beyond repair with three hours of the race to go. I was totally gutted. I'd had less than four hours sleep in two days and felt like shit and the last thing I'd wanted was to be paraded into a hospitality suite to meet some potential sponsors - VIPs from some big accountancy firm. Six months later we were married. I'd trusted my instincts then, knowing it was the right thing to do. We were in love. I also knew when she'd tired of me, or perhaps my unwillingness to embrace her world. Her affair merely confirmed that our love affair was over.

She was already married when we met, but only in theory. The decree absolute came through six weeks before the wedding. Sinead is married, but it all seems a bit tenuous. She's admitted that they've got problems and any fool can see that they're totally unsuited to one another.

Sinead's also about my age or maybe a bit younger. I didn't think that marrying an older woman would be a problem until I mentioned children. I didn't think that I'd want children, but that was another feeling I couldn't deny. When I tried to talk about it, she'd dismissed the idea and said that she was too old to have children and wanted to concentrate on her career without any distractions.

I did know however, that as soon as we met we were both attracted to each other. The closest I've got to Sinead is that she thinks I'm sweet. Last night I was thrilled, but at five o'clock in the morning, sweet is pleasant, nice, ineffectual... Hardly strong enough emotions to start a love affair. After all, I've no reason to believe that Sinead is interested in me. She's probably desperately in love with her husband and fighting to keep their marriage intact.

I need to understand my feelings, but also accept that this isn't going anywhere. I've got to concentrate on the eight hundred or so miles ahead of me and the immediate problem of today's one hundred and fifteen mile ride.

Half an hour later I'm slipping back to sleep, but the force behind the morning wake up makes sure it doesn't happen.

'It's just another manic Monday, I wish it were a Sunday, 'Cause that's my fun day, My I don't have to run day, It's just another manic Monday'.

I'd forgotten it was Monday. The days are merging into one.

It's a sad sight. In front of the admin tent four people are standing in a line. A young guy with a massive cotton wool pad taped over his left eye, an overweight woman who would struggle to get on a bike let alone ride it, a girl supporting herself on a pair of crutches and Mike.

He smiles when he sees me. "You don't know what a relief it was to wake up this morning to that stupid bloody music and then realise that I didn't have to get on that sodding bike."

Mike explains that they're waiting for a taxi to take them to Fort William station. From there he has a somewhat convoluted mixture of train journeys which, with a bit of luck, should get him back to Illfracombe before midnight. I ask him how his bike is getting back and he says that he's told them to dump it. I think he's joking, but don't pursue it. I'm about to say another goodbye, when I have an idea.

"Mike, can you do me a favour?" I say.

"If I can."

"You know that you're good at finding ladies on the Internet. Can you do a search and see if you can find out anything about a woman cyclist called Sinead O'Connor?"

Mike pulls a face. "Not the singer," I say. "She might have been an Irish professional or a good amateur, maybe ten or so years ago."

"I'll see what I can do," Mike answers.

I say that I'll try and ring him tomorrow night to see if he's found out anything. We have a final man hug - this is getting a habit.

I'm waiting at the edge of the queue looking for Sinead. I know what I told her last night, but I need to see her. They've already opened the start and people are moving past me. I'm wasting precious time.

Five minutes later, I'm about to give up when I see her coming out of the bike compound with Lawrence and I walk over to them. Lawrence nods and Sinead pretends to ignore me, looking away into the bike compound. I haven't got time to mess about.

"You might need these," I say.

I give her the tyre levers I'd picked up yesterday when she had the puncture.

Without waiting for a reply I turn and head for the start line. I can play hard to get too! Or am I just desperate to get going?

There's bad news at the start line briefing. Due to road closures around Glasgow, the route has had to be changed which adds another ten miles. Great! We've now got to ride one hundred and twenty five miles and to make things worse it's beginning to rain.

Fort William is quiet as we cycle through the town. The rain is real Scotch mist; thick soaking drizzle and Ben Nevis has disappeared under a grey shroud of cloud. On the edge of the town there is a row of B&Bs, guest houses and hotels facing Loch Linnhe. Rider's friends and families staying in them have left their breakfasts to line the road, clapping and cheering as we ride by. They don't just clap people they know, they clap everyone, which temporarily makes the rain feel less wet and cold.

The black 4x4 passes and turns left into a hotel car park. As I get level with the entrance, Sinead's husband is walking into the hotel. No doubt he wants his breakfast and hasn't got the time or inclination to clap as we ride past.

The first twenty five miles or so are not too bad. The A82 runs alongside Loch Linnhe and rises and falls like the Loch Ness road, but with friendlier gradients and no skinny dippers to distract the female riders. We sweep down through the tunnel of steelwork which creates a bridge between Loch Linnhe and Loch Leven and ride towards the village of Glencoe. Just before the village there's a mini pit stop. Unlike the other pit stops, it's not compulsory to stop and I decide that because I started late, I'll ride on. After it's only twenty five miles to the next one!

We start to climb into Glen Coe. We climb and then we climb and climb again. It must be about five miles before the road begins to level out, but it hasn't been too steep, well not killer steep, just long.

A group of riders speed past and it's no surprise to see Lawrence in the middle. A bike comes alongside and Sinead smiles. "Thanks for the tyre levers and I must say you look very co-ordinated."

Flattered, I reply, "Well I haven't been riding that long."

She laughs. "No, I don't mean your riding, I mean your colours are co-ordinated. Red and white bike, red and white shoes and a red and white helmet."

I'd had to buy all my gear at once so it was easy to make sure colours matched. I not going to admit to the red and black jersey under my yellow waterproof jacket.

"Oh, I forgot the red and black jersey you were wearing yesterday," she adds. "See you later."

She gets out of the saddle and sprints away, her bum rocking from side to side. I'm convinced that the scorpion is waving at me with a smug look on its face.

'See you later'. Perhaps things aren't that bad.

After another five miles of barren undulating countryside, I realise that I'm thinking that Glen Coe is a hill or mountain and I'm expecting to descend at any time, but it's just a long bloody drag to nowhere.

The visibility has dropped as fast as the temperature; it's May yet it feels like January. Scotch mist has turned into Scotch fog and I can barely see thirty yards ahead. I'm not alone in not having any lights on the bike. I'd dismissed the organisers advice to bring lights as overkill, but am regretting it as cars, lorries and coaches emerge from the gloom on the narrow road.

Two medic motorbikes speed past. Despite the fog, they're travelling faster than they usually do and their blue lights are flashing.

We're now cycling in open moorland on the edge of Rannoch Moor. The landscape looks black and dismal and is interspersed with patches of silvery grey where lakes of water break up the expanse of gorse and heather. We pass a solitary hotel at one of the highest points and I ask myself who in their right mind would choose to stay there?

The road descends rapidly in a series of twists and turns and the fog becomes less dense as we get lower. In the distance I can just make out the blue flashing lights of the medic motorbikes reflecting off the mist. I'm not sure, but they seem to be stationary. I then make out a homogenous mass of yellow jackets and bikes and it's not long before the shout '*slow down accident*' is passed up the line of cyclist. There's a high pitched whine as brake pads work hard to slow everyone's descent.

Sinead was riding ahead and despite the cold, I feel a clammy sweat.

I stop with around fifty riders about thirty yards from the motorbikes. A wail of sirens resonates around the moors, but it's impossible to tell how close they are. Nobody is saying anything. On a raised bank by the side of the road ahead, I can see someone sitting with their head in their hands. The shape of their body and posture makes me think that it's Lawrence, but I can't be sure. Sinead was behind Lawrence, but I can't see her.

I push my way forward, explaining that I can see a friend who's been hurt. Half the road is closed off by roadworks controlled by traffic lights and the road is strewn with bent and broken bikes. Three people are lying by the side of the road and are being tended by the medics, one is screaming in pain. I try to see what they're wearing, praying I don't see a scorpion.

The man on the bank is Lawrence and he's still got his head in his hands. One of his arms is a mass of grazes and cuts from his shoulder to his forearm and his right thigh is bleeding from a deeper cut.

"Lawrence, are you okay?"

He looks up, shaking with shock and cold. He's not wearing a jacket so I take mine off and hold it out to him. I'm not sure whether he recognises me or not, but ignores the jacket. I wrap it around his shoulders.

He starts talking uncharacteristically loudly. "What a fucking prat. What the hell did he think he was doing? He's fucked everything up."

"What happened?" I ask gently, whilst glancing across at the riders being tended. As far as I can make out, they're all men and I relax a bit.

Lawrence doesn't need to be asked twice and becomes agitated. "We were all in a group coming down quickly and could see the traffic lights. It was obvious that they'd be green when we got to them, so we all slowed down and moved over to go through the open bit of road. Then arsehole features decides that he's going to get ahead and carries on through the coned off bit. It didn't look like they'd done anything to the road, but towards the end, he hits a trench and goes over the handlebars. His bike shot sideways into the path of us other guys and it's fucking carnage." He casts a venomous look towards a man sat by the side of the road. The man doesn't look hurt. "Of course he gets thrown sideways into a load of gorse and heather and comes out with hardly a scratch," Lawrence adds.

The man being looked after by the medics screams again and my stomach churns. "Is he badly hurt?" I ask.

"I think - I hope it's just his collar bone, maybe a few cracked ribs. Pain's not such a bad thing. It's the internal injuries you can't feel that will kill you."

Two ambulances and a police car have pushed their way through the crowd. "Go on Lawrence, " I say. "Go and get yourself sorted out, you'll be back on the road in no time."

"You are joking aren't you, have you seen my bike? The forks are totally knackered and the frame's cracked. I know those bike mechanics are good, but they can't work miracles."

I smile weakly. "Sinead, the girl you were riding with," I ask, "I haven't seen her, is she alright do you know?"

"Yes, she was in the group ahead and missed it all. She's probably in Glasgow by now."

I'm walking off and Lawrence calls after me, holding out my jacket. "You'll need this - thanks," he says.

Just how long can fifteen miles be? I know it's a ridiculous question, but I glare at my bike computer willing each tenth of a mile on. My rough calculation made it fifteen miles from the accident to the first pit stop. It feels like I've already ridden twenty, but the computer shows that there's still another ten to go. The terrain is a monotonous mixture of moorland, forest, water and rock. Stuff scenery! I want supermarkets, offices, houses......civilisation.

I think the cold and wet is affecting my brain. The road looks as if slopes downhill, but it feels like I'm cycling uphill. I check the computer and it confirms a two per cent uphill gradient. So my legs are telling me the truth, but my eyes are lying to me. It's bad enough cycling uphill when my whole body is in agreement, but it's a damn sight more difficult when two major components are in disagreement. To make things worse, the tarmac road surface has been worn away to expose a washboard of raised granite chippings which do their best to resist every revolution of the wheels.

At long, long last, it's the final sweeping bend down to the first pit stop at a place called Tyndrum. A marshall with a broad Scottish accent and loud voice welcomes and congratulates me. I feel better when he confirms that it was a very tough ride in the fog and rain. He even knows what I'm talking about when I describe the downhill optical illusion of the last ten miles. A bit like chocolate fudge bars and salami sticks, I'd never have believed that I'd find comfort in a loud Scotsman.

There are a lot of bikes at the pit stop but very few people. I need the toilet and go into a cafe next to the stop. The place is heaving with cold, wet cyclists and I'm immediately hit by a blast of damp heat. Condensation streams down the windows due to the water vapour coming from so many soaked bodies. I want to stay, get warm, have a cup of coffee and eat countless pies, but know that if I do, there's a very real chance I'll never get back on the bike. It's nearly one o'clock and with seventy five miles to go, I've still got a lot of riding to do. I force myself back out through the door, grab a pork pie, a packet of crisps and a banana from the food station outside and scoff them down standing by my bike.

Someone calls my name. It's Gillian who's come out of the cafe holding a cup of coffee.

"I thought I saw you," she says. "We're off in a minute, are you going to join us?"

It's not difficult to work out who *'we'* are.

Bob has now followed her out of the cafe.

Gillian says, "Look who I've found Bob. Mark is going to ride with us."

My eyes meet Gillian's. She raises her eyelids and her body language says, *'please ride with us, I can't stand much more of this prick',* or words to that effect.

I don't reply. Bob grunts and is far from happy.

Afternoon....

I need to turn my brain off and stop thinking. I can't cycle the next seventy five miles staring at the bike computer as it registers each fraction of a mile. I switch it off, look at my watch and do some simple mathematics. On a good day, I can ride fairly long distances at an average of between fourteen and fifteen miles and on a bad day it will drop to between twelve and thirteen, but no slower. So if I set myself a minimum speed of twelve miles an hour, I should be back at the base camp at around seven o'clock. That's fine. Still enough time for a chocolate fudge and salami stick snack, a Posh Wash and something to eat. All I have to do is keep turning my legs for the next six hours and I'll finish.

Bob has got the hump and assumes the role of lead cyclist. I'm slowly learning the weird and wonderful world of serious group cycling. At first, I thought I'd inadvertently encountered a strange sect who communicated by way of secret hand signals. Bob has clearly been inducted into the cyclist's secret sign society. The one he uses most is the hand down, fingers outstretched sign which means pothole in the road. Bob obviously possesses some extra sensory power that enables him to see potholes which are totally invisible to Gillian and myself. He uses the pointed finger behind the back sign when a large immovable object such as a parked car is in the road ahead. Without him, we would of course, ride straight into the immovable object, in the same way that lemmings throw themselves off cliffs to a certain death. It strikes me that constantly taking your hands on and off the handlebars is inherently far more dangerous than any pothole or parked car.

Accompanying the hand signals is the cyclist's shout, something which comes as second nature to Bob. A car is such an unusual thing to encounter on a road, that he is unable to resist shouting and telling us about it. He shouts either *'Car Up'* or *'Car Down'* depending on the direction the car is travelling. This is so useful for Gillian and myself who have obviously lost the power of sight. Bob must also believe that we don't get out much. He shouts that a large four legged animal with a rider on its back is a *'horse'* and that a large motorised vehicle with knobbly tyres is a *'tractor'*. Best of all is when he gets to traffic lights. He tells us to *'stop'* at a red light and to *'go'* at a green light. I'm at a loss to know how I cycle without him and remain alive.

There are twenty five miles to go and Bob's still shouting and pointing like he's got some neurological complaint. Gillian is quiet and suffering in dignified silence. Every few miles she drops back a bit and needs to rest after climbing long hills.

Once again I resort to grumpiness to cope with my tiredness. I'm grumpy about Bob and his incessant shouting, Glasgow's Highways Department for closing roads, the second pit stop crew for not knowing that I have to have three chocolate fudge bars in the afternoon and trying to pass off Kit Kats as a suitable alternative.......The list goes on.

After a while my grumpiness turns to anger and I start on *her*. Had *she* not tired of me and started an affair, there wouldn't have been a divorce and I wouldn't be here in the first place. *She's* probably travelling business class somewhere whilst I'm killing myself slogging along some badly
maintained Scottish road.

There's a *'RED'* light at a road junction and I crack.

I shout. "WHEN CAN WE TAKE THE FUCKING STABILISERS OFF OUR BIKES?"

79

Stupid I know and maybe unfair. Bob's way of dealing with the miles is to take charge. But my outburst makes me feel better. Gillian smiles and Bob chooses to ignore me.

The lights change - 'GO'. I pedal on.

Evening....

My rudimentary calculation proves remarkably accurate and the three of us roll over the finish line, somewhere north of Glasgow, at six forty five.

On the way back from my Posh Wash, I drop two pairs of shorts and a jersey off at the laundry. They've even got a portable laundry in a tent in a field, how good is that! You leave your stuff in the evening and by six o'clock the next morning it's washed, put in a numbered bag and hung up in numerical order on lines in the tent. I think about asking if they do a home service - they can pitch their tent in my back garden.

Walking back, I make a detour to where the low numbered tents are pitched. Lawrence is sitting outside one of them with his arm and leg heavily bandaged. He's scribbling something on a piece of A3 paper which is covered with writing, circles and arrows. I crouch down with great difficulty and fear that I won't be able to get up again.

He tells me that they'd taken the injured and walking wounded back to a hospital in Fort

William. Lawrence had been cleaned up and discharged. The guy in pain had broken his collar bone and is being kept in. The two other injured riders are also being kept in for observation overnight, but Lawrence didn't think they had any serious injuries.

Lawrence's demeanour has changed from the angry man I'd spoken to earlier; he's sullen and hardly looks up when he's talking. I point to the piece of paper. "Is that your blog of the ride?"

"No."

The conversation stalls and there's an awkward silence before he waves the piece of paper in the air. "This is my life, although I'm not quite sure where to start today."

"So it's some kind of diary?" I ask.

There's another short silence before Lawrence looks up and stares at me. It's quite disconcerting and I wonder what he's about to say.

"My wife left me," he says.

It sounds familiar. How many people are doing this ride after their marriage has screwed up?

Lawrence continues. "I didn't cope too well - went under a bit. They taught me to do this." He holds the paper out. "I map out my day, who I've met and what I've done. Then I write down how I felt at the time and try and rationalise those feelings."

I feel a bit embarrassed, I'm not sure I want to know about all of this, but Lawrence seems like he wants to talk and after the day he's had, I think the least I can do is listen.

"It's about training your mind not to jump to the wrong conclusions. If someone doesn't say good morning to you, you might immediately assume that they don't like you, but they may not notice you because there're worrying about something and are pre-occupied. Or maybe they're just short sighted."

I want to lighten the conversation and point to the paper. "So am I on there?"

He points to a small circle which is linked by a line to a big circle in the middle.

"Yes, that's you and the big circle is the crash. Everything will point to the crash today."

"And what does it say about me? Nothing too bad I hope."

Lawrence peers over his glasses. "No, it says - *'Mark, nice guy, lends me jacket'*. So when I read that, it makes me think that not all of the world is against me."

And I thought I was maudlin!

With a great deal of effort I manage to get myself up and try to ignore the shooting pain in my knee.

"Have you eaten?" I ask.

Lawrence nods.

"Well, I must go and get something to eat. There's a bar in the chill-out area tonight and I need a beer after today's ride. So if you fancy a drink, I'll see you there about nine."

"No thanks, I'll finish this."

"Come on, it'll do you good, "I say.

Lawrence doesn't reply and starts writing again.

I meet Gillian in the food tent when I'm having dinner and try to persuade her to have a drink, but she looks all-in and I'm not surprised when she says that she wants to go to bed. It's half past nine and I decide to have quick drink and go to bed.

There aren't many people in the chill-out area and I head towards the bar which comprises a cloth covered trestle table with three aluminium barrels on it. Behind, a domestic fridge holds a couple of bottles of white wine and some bottles of Coke.

I'm thirsty and ask for two bottles of coke in a glass. The barman asks in a broad Glaswegian accent if I'd like ice. I say no and he puts a single bottle of Coke into a glass and fills it up with ice. I don't say anything. It's obviously a language thing.

Lawrence comes over holding an empty beer glass.

"Mark, I changed my mind, let me buy you a drink."

He's talking loudly and I suspect that Lawrence is not used to drinking and that the pint he's just finished has already taken effect. I've already finished my very cold Coke and accept his offer. He buys two pints and we sit down at a table.

There's no need for me to start the conversation.

"Might as well drink. I think I'll head home tomorrow," he says.

"Why? Surely they'll lend you a bike - they've got spare ones."

He scoffs. "Have you seen them? Real bone shakers."

I want to tell him that the spare bikes are the same model as mine, but resist. When you're as good a rider as he is, I can understand wanting the best machinery. I always must have the best car for a race.

I don't want him to give up.

"Come on, what's the point in going back and what will you do? Go back to work? You won't be able to go cycling because you've haven't got a bike."

Wrong!

"I've got five other bikes at home," he says.

I persevere. "Well why not try one of their bikes? Give it a day or so and see how it goes?"

Lawrence is thinking. "But I won't be able to ride with the quick guys, even if the bike's all right, I'm going to be stiff and these bandages won't make it easy."

"Does that matter? It's not a race. Look up, enjoy the scenery, help slower people like me."

Christ! I'm beginning to sound evangelical.

"You try telling some of them that it's not a race," Lawrence replies. "There's a lot of riders wanting to post the fastest time. Not that I'm going to do that, some of them are ex-professionals and national amateurs, but I really wanted to finish in the top thirty."

I try to think of more reasons why he shouldn't give up, but he remains unconvinced. We chat and I tell him about my divorce and aided by his two pints and my one pint, we have a bit of a laugh and swap divorce stories. We get to the awkward point when our glasses are empty. I really should offer to buy another drink, but I want to go to bed and I fear what might happen if Lawrence has any more.

There's a lull in the conversation before Lawrence says. "She's a funny girl."

"Who?" I ask.

"The girl you know, Sinead."

"Why?"

"Well, she's a bloody good cyclist. I reckon she might have been professional at some time. So why's she doing this? She's not doing it with anyone else. She told me that her husband is with her, but I've never seen him. He's not at any of pit stops or by the side of road like the other supporters."

I don't tell him that he's echoing my thoughts. Lawrence continues.

"And why the hell does she get up so early in the morning?"

"What do you mean?"

"I hear her every morning - she's up at four thirty. By the time I surface, she's gone. Tent all cleared, the lot. God knows where she goes and I've never seen her at breakfast. The lawyer in me tells me it's all a bit strange."

Night...

How many times am I going to tell myself that I'm not going to be awake at four thirty and staring out of my tent flap watching for Sinead in order to see where she goes?

I remember that I haven't rung Mike to see if he managed to found out anything about her. It's quarter to eleven and I convince myself that it's not too late to ring.

No reply.

Then it dawns on me. When did I say goodbye to Mike, was it yesterday or this morning?

Shit! It was this morning. He won't even be home yet.

I close my eyes. It's been a long day.

Day Four

Morning...

"Did you enjoy The Proclaimers?" Gillian asks.

What the hell is she talking about? I've just joined her in the start queue and am barely awake.

She persists. "You know, '*I will walk five hundred miles, I will walk five hundred mooore*'. The wake-up call." Her attempt at a Scottish accent makes me smile and I'm pleased that she looks a lot better than she did last night. I explain that at five thirty I was fast asleep. In fact I was still fast asleep at six o'clock. So much for being awake at four thirty to spy on Sinead.

My knee is hurting and I take the weight off my right leg, but the pain doesn't go away.

Gillian looks around. "You will ride with us today won't you? I know I'm a bit slow, but..."

She doesn't need to finish the sentence.

"Why don't you just tell him to piss off. Sorry about the language, but you know what I mean," I reply.

"Well I'm tempted, but it's probably not the sort of language a vicar's wife should use."

Without thinking I say, "But I thought you said that your husband had rowed the Atlantic."

She laughs. "The two things aren't mutually exclusive you know and if you're going to row the

Atlantic, having the big boss on your side is not a bad thing."

A vision fills my blurred head and I'm tempted to ask if her husband plays the organ. I'm tempted, but resist.

"So where's our leader this morning?" I ask instead.

"Oh don't worry. I'm sure he'll be here soon," Gillian replies.

Bobby Big Bollocks (the name came to me suddenly) is leading us over the start line when another rider pushes in from the side. I'm about to have my first strop of the day when I see that he's got bandages on his arm and thigh.

"Do you mind if I join you?" Lawrence asks.

The first challenge of the day is to get from the north of Glasgow to the south. I'm convinced it can't be done without at least a glimpse of a tenement building, a Rangers or Celtic supporter or a motorway, but I'm proved wrong. The route planners have devised a route that cleverly circumnavigates the hub of the city, however, the bad news is that they haven't managed to avoid the bland satellite towns of Bothwell, Hamilton and Larkhill.

As it's the beginning of the day's ride and there haven't been any open roads to allow the quicker riders to get ahead, there are large numbers of cyclists bunched together causing rush hour mayhem in the congested towns. Although most ride in single or double file, some groups fill the whole of one side of the road. When the traffic lights are red, we all edge past the stationary traffic and collect in a large bunch at the front of the queue, which means that the cars behind are stuck behind a mass of bikes when the lights change. Most motorists are fine, but a few get annoyed. They've probably only got fifteen minutes of their journey left before spending the day in their comfortable offices, whereas we've got nearly a hundred miles in front of us and need to get on. We are hardly acknowledged or noticed by early morning shoppers, but school children on their way to school wave and give us the thumbs up. This is spoilt when a spotty pubescent youth decides to spit at us. Maybe he's expressing empathy with the motorists.

Our trinity, or if I include Lawrence, our quartet, is broken up by the traffic. I know that Bob and Lawrence are ahead as they quickly adopted the more aggressive style of urban cycling, but I have no idea where Gillian is. I consider stopping, but she could possibly be in front and so I carry on. The larger towns give way to smaller ones until we are back in the open countryside again; countryside which is dissected by the M74, the main artery for traffic travelling between England and Scotland. We of course cannot use the motorway, so take the B7076 which runs alongside the motorway for mile after monotonous mile. The road was presumably the motorway's predecessor and appears to have had

89

no maintenance since the motorway was built. It also has very little traffic no doubt because, very sensibly, it's all on the super smooth motorway.

The monotony is broken when the route signs direct us off the B7076 and into the small and unremarkable town of Crawford for our first pit stop. I can see the banners for the stop a couple of hundred yards ahead on the right hand side, but before that, on the left hand side is a primary school. The entire school is lining the edge of the road and I can't imagine what interpretation of the National Curriculum, or whatever the Scottish equivalent is, makes waving, clapping and cheering a bunch of passing cyclists a compliant lesson. Some children step into the road and tap us on the shoulder as we pass and I wonder how the teachers dealt with the lesson plan and risk assessment. *'Sorry Mrs McDonald, but Hamish was run down by ten cyclists during this morning's spelling test'.* It's great to see them and temporarily takes my mind off the increasingly worrying pain in my thigh and knee.

Bob and Lawrence are at the pit stop, but there's no sign of Gillian. Bob's words and manner are accusatory. He'd *'assumed'* that I was looking after Gillian and had he known that I wasn't, he'd have dropped back. I'm relieved when she rides into the stop about five minutes later, but then feel guilty when I notice that her face is drawn and pale. She explains that she finds traffic the hardest bit of cycling and is terrified riding through built up areas and busy roads. Having ridden or driven on two or four wheels almost all of my life on all kinds of roads, I've never considered that negotiating traffic is anything other than an irritating hassle, but realise that to someone who has done their riding in the country, it must be pretty daunting. I resolve to make sure that Gillian is looked after in the future, but Bob's body language leaves me in no doubt that he has no intention of leaving her wellbeing in my hands.

Lawrence is distracted by a group of riders who have ridden in to the pit stop and rushes over to them as soon as they stop. Sinead is amongst them and I want to go over and speak to her, but decide that I'm no more than the sweet guy who helps with a puncture. They get off their bikes, take a bit of food, fill their water bottles and then they're off. I feel sorry for Lawrence as he watches them go. It must be like me pulling out of a major motor race and having to accept a red letter day birthday drive as a replacement. I hope he doesn't give up on us.

The next stop is thirty seven miles away and Gillian must wish that she'd never admitted to any kind of weakness as Bob sticks to her like a leach, despite the only traffic being the occasional tractor and postman's van. Lawrence intermittently shoots ahead alone, but then drops back. Unable to separate Bob and Gillian, he cycles with me and I'm surprised how easily we chat. He's totally at home on a bike, as it seems to be one of the few things that come easily to him. My knee is hurting like hell and I'm aware that I'm slowing down, but somehow the four of us stick together; a disparate collection of riders, ebbing and flowing, but never too far apart.

Afternoon....

The B7076 road is endless. It is the road to hell, or more accurately the road of hell. We skirt past Lockerbie and I know that we must be somewhere near the border with England. Lockerbie is such a familiar name that I want to see the scars and memorials first hand, but the route signs guide us past and on to the next stop five miles north of Gretna Green.

A mile before the stop, the Trans-Global circus passes. First the team car, then the peloton of riders and finally two estate cars with their roofs crammed with spare bikes. Lawrence looks in awe as they pass and I have to admit that their speed and the way they ride in such a precise and ordered group is pretty amazing. I ask Lawrence how fast they're travelling and he guesses around thirty five miles an hour. My bike computer shows that I'm just about maintaining fourteen miles an hour.

We pick up food at the pit stop and I stuff a salami stick and two chocolate fudge bars into my pocket for my tent feast later. The four of us sit on a grass verge in silence, each of lost in our own thoughts and too tired to chat. One of the escort motorbikes is parked nearby.

"That sign on the front of the bike really annoys me," I say.

Bob bites. "Why?"

"Well it says '*Slow Bike Event',* but I don't think we're *that* slow."

Gillian and Lawrence laugh. Bob is silent for a second or two. "No, it doesn't mean that, it's telling approaching traffic to slow down."

I catch Gillian's eye and smile. "And some they fell on stony ground," I say.

"Matthew Chapter 13 Verse 5," she replies.

Bob looks confused.

Outside Gretna Green, we have a group discussion. The route misses the Old Blacksmith's Shop and Gillian and I want to take a look whereas Bob and Lawrence want to press on. There's about thirty miles to the finish just south of Carlisle and there's no reason why we can't split up, but Bob is fussing about Gillian getting through the Carlisle traffic. She eagerly assures him that she'll be fine, presumably preferring to take her chances with a thirty five ton juggernaut rather than spend more miles with Bob for sole company. In the end Lawrence goes on alone and the three of us head towards the Old Blacksmith's Shop.

Gretna Green appears to have taken its style, or lack of it, from John O'Groats and Land's End. God it's tacky. We don't stay long. Just long enough for me to take a photo of Bob and Gillian by the obligatory Scottish piper. It's a difficult photo to take because Gillian is constantly squirming as Bob insists on putting his arm around her back and squeezing her. I take one more photo of Gillian by herself under a wrought iron arch with horseshoes welded to it. I get down on my knees and propose to her, but immediately regret it. Not because she rejects me, but due to the agonising pain as I get up. Before we leave, I text the picture of Gillian under the arch to Mike.

Just outside Gretna Green, I see one of the most welcome signs I've ever seen - *'Welcome to England'*. I'm staggered that it's taken us three and a half days to cycle out of Scotland. I understand Scotland now - a beautiful top, an ugly middle and a boring bottom. The sign is almost totally obscured by the large number of cyclists draped over it and having their photograph taken. We decide against another photo and head towards Carlisle.

Luckily the late Tuesday afternoon traffic isn't too heavy and Bob leads Gillian easily through the city whilst I ride shotgun at the back.

By the time we finish, I know that I must get some physio on my knee if I'm going to stand any chance of riding tomorrow. Forgetting about a cup of tea and Posh Wash, I make my way to the physio and massage tent.

It's going to be a long wait. I've been given a ticket by the girl behind the desk and told to wait until my number's called. It's a bit like being at a Tesco deli counter. There's no room in the small waiting area, so I sit on the grass outside. There's a bit of heat left in the late afternoon sun and soon I'm lying down, eyes closed and feeling myself dozing off.

Somebody's gently kicking my leg, luckily it's the left one, and I open my eyes, shielding them from the sun with my hand.

It's Sinead.

"Hi," she says, "what's the problem?"

I explain about my leg.

"Stand up."

It sounds like an order so I struggle up. She prods and pulls my knee and then runs her hand up the outside of my thigh.

"It's your IT band. How long have you been waiting?"

"About an hour."

She looks at the queue and then across to the car park. "Come on. I'll sort you out."

I'm not sure what my face looks like, but she says, "Don't look so worried. I won't hurt you. I've sorted hundreds of IT bands out, but we need to be quick."

Without waiting for a reply, she walks off and I follow.

We get to her tent. She looks around quickly and dives inside. I stand there motionless. She sticks her head out of the flap and there's a sense of urgency in her voice. "Don't just stand there, get inside."

I crawl in head first and breathe in the feminine air, a mix of perfume, make-up and whatever other potions and creams women use. Sinead is sitting cross legged on one side of the tent. She's wearing shorts and a tee shirt. I know it sounds as if I'm obsessed with nipples, but Sinead's not wearing a bra and her nipples are gently pressing through the thin fabric of her tee shirt. They're not organ stops, more small pert buttons.

She ushers me to one side as she rolls out a sleeping bag. "Right, get your shorts off," she says.

I'm wearing bib shorts and need to remove my jersey in order to get them off, which means that I'll be naked apart from my socks and the name tag around my neck.

"But...." I utter.

"For Christ's sake, stop faffing about. I can't sort your knee out if you've got your shorts on. I'm a nurse for God's sake, there's nothing I haven't seen before, "she says.

My response should be, *well you haven't seen mine before*, but I'm finding speech difficult.

She throws me a towel. "If it makes you feel better, I'll turn my back and you can protect your modesty with this."

Sinead shuffles around so her back is turned as I struggle out of my jersey and shorts. I remember I haven't had a shower.

"I didn't get a chance to have a shower so I'm probably a bit smelly," I say.

"I've smelt worse, now just get on with it."

I'm not sure if I should lie on my back or front and opt for my back, at least I can see what she's doing. I'm not showing off or anything, but it's a small towel and I take a bit of time to place it strategically.

"Okay," I say.

She shuffles back round. "About time. I haven't got any proper massage oil, so we'll have to make do with baby oil."

Life's a bitch sometimes.

"Which leg is it?" she says. "Roll over on your side with the bad leg facing upwards."

Sinead is on my left hand side and I need to roll towards her, which means my front will be facing her. Why couldn't it be my left leg? I move gently on to my side whilst trying to keep the towel in place. I fail and the towel slips down. I grab it and put it back, but it slips down again.

Sinead giggles.

I remember the skinny dippers and the disparaging remark made by the girl in the food queue and want to make some excuse about the compressing effect of tight cycling shorts.

Sod it! I give up. Maybe she is a nurse.

She picks up the towel, places it over me and pats in place. She rubs oil into her hands and starts to manipulate my knee. I look at her face - Christ, her eyes are beautiful.

After a few minutes, she says, "Now this might hurt a little, be brave."

The bony part of her hand where it meets her wrist is buried into the top of my thigh and drawn down towards my knee. Her other hand pushes down on her wrist adding more pressure.

Shit it hurts! My leg flexes with the pain and the towel slips off again, but I'm past caring. She replaces the towel and pushes down again and then again. If it hurt before, it certainly does now.

"Well let's see how that works, we might need to do it again tomorrow," she says calmly.

I'm torn - do I want it to get better or not?

Sinead gently pushes me over onto my back and without saying anything starts massaging my back and shoulders. My hand moves and touches her leg. I stroke her leg. She doesn't make any attempt to move and her hands slide slowly up and down my back. Neither of us say anything.

A part of my body which I thought had stopped working a long time ago comes to life.

I feel a drop of water on my back and then another. Her hands stop moving and I turn over, grab the towel and place it over me - well more hang it over me.

Sinead is staring ahead with tears running down her cheeks. I lean forward and hold out my arms. She holds me tightly, almost clinging.

After a few minutes, I pull her away from me. "Are you going to tell me what this is all about?" I ask.

She scrubs away the tears. "What do you mean?"

"I think you know what."

"Don't be stupid, I'm a bit tired that's all."

A phone rings and a look of alarm spreads across her face. She throws the contents of the tent around looking for the phone, but by the time she's found it it's stopped ringing. Without looking to see who's rung, she redials. She makes it clear that our tryst is over by animatedly gesturing for me to put my clothes back on. As I do, I try and make out what is being said on the phone.

'I'm still in the tent..... yes sorry I didn't realise the time........... dropped off to sleep........ yes I'll be there as quickly as possible'.

The call ends and she pushes me out of the tent. There's a guy sitting outside an adjacent tent who smiles wryly as we emerge. I want to say that it's not what it seems, but think why? It might have been.

Sinead walks off and I try to keep up with her. She turns.

"For god's sake, please go away, you've got to leave me alone."

I stop and watch her walk away towards the car park, the 4x4 and the Trans Global motorhome.

Evening....

Mike finally picks up his phone. "Mike. It's Mark from the ride."

"Mark good to hear from you, where are you?"

Shit! Where are we? My mind is blank. I'm no longer in the real world, the roads, the hills, the buildings, the base camps....they've all merged into one. I then remember.

"Carlisle, somewhere south of Carlisle. How was your journey home?"

I listen impatiently as Mike relates the detail of his tortuous journey home. He then wants to know about the last two day's riding, so I tell him about the accident, about Lawrence, about Bob and Gillian.

"You look after my Gillian," he says, "I think she's got a soft spot for you."

I think about it and conclude that as lovely as she is, she'll always remind me of my mother.

Finally, I manage to steer the conversation around to what he's been able to find out about Sinead.

"No problem, he replies. " There's loads of stuff about her. She's an Irish singer with very short hair."

My heart sinks and there's a moment's silence before I hear Mike chuckle.

"Nice one Mike, you had me going. Did you manage to find out anything about Sinead O'Connor, the cyclist?"

"Yes, but not as much as the singer," he replies and laughs again. "Sorry I'll be serious. You were right, there is an Irish cyclist called Sinead O'Connor who won two consecutive Irish Road Race titles in 1999 and 2000. She then joined an Irish professional team, but they went bust in 2003 and after that the trail goes cold. Oh yes, she married another professional rider called Danny Doyle in 2000."

"Danny, not Richard?"

"No I'm sure it was Danny."

I thank Mike and promise to ring him in a couple of days to let him know how things are going.

"Oh, one final thing," he says, "Thanks for the text and picture - they are magnificent."

He's still laughing as he puts the phone down.

I'm clearing the remains of my dinner into the rubbish bin when I notice Sinead by the food tent entrance. She's not alone.

As I walk out, I smile at Sinead and her husband Richard. His leg comes out and effectively blocks my way. He holds his hand out.

"Mark isn't it? Sinead tells me you've got a bad knee. That's the last thing you want on a ride like this."

I shake his hand, correctly anticipating his attempt to break each of my fingers.

"Sinead and I were going to have a drink in the chill-out tent," he says, "why don't you join us?"

I mumble an excuse about an early night and wanting to rest my knee, but he grabs my shoulder. "No I insist, we need to get to know one another better."

He leads me to the chill-out tent. Sinead walks behind.

"So what do you do?" He asks. He's bought some drinks and we're sitting around a small table.

"I'm in motorsport," I reply. I don't expect him to let it go.

"Oh that's interesting, do you drive?"

"When I can," I reply, "but it's all about sponsorship and money and there's not a lot of it about."

"So are you good? Should I have heard of you?"

"I'm okay, but you won't have heard of me."

I look at Sinead, but she's avoiding my eyes. Her fingers are nervously spinning a wedding ring on her left hand. She hasn't worn rings before and I'd assumed that she didn't wear them for fear of losing them whilst riding. There's another ring on her left hand and two on her right hand, but unlike the wedding ring which is bright yellow gold, the other rings are either white gold or platinum. The wedding ring just doesn't look right and the way she's spinning it, it looks too big for her finger.

I look at my left hand. The ring of white skin where my ring was has now gone. On the palm of my hand is a number - my tent number. I ask the girls to write it on my hand, because as soon as they tell me my number, I immediately forget it.

Richard is not going to stop probing. "Come on you're just being modest. What have you won - ever done Formula One?"

"I've won couple of race series, but haven't done Formula One."

"You're not good enough then?"

I could tell him that Formula One has got very little to do with talent and lot to do with how rich your Daddy is and whether he bought you a go-kart at the age of six months. I could also tell him that I was probably a bit too bright. F1 drivers are better if they don't have too much of a brain and can function as automatons in highly sophisticated bits of machinery.

Instead I reply, "Something like that."

He doesn't give up. "So what do you do when you're not driving?"

I get up. "I'm a second hand car dealer - now I really need to go to bed."

Richard stands up and his hand locks on my shoulder again.

"Did you hear that darling? Mark's really a second car dealer. I don't think he's a racing driver at all."

His hand squeezes my shoulder blade. He's a strong guy.

"So you can forget sniffing around Sinead, she's high maintenance and won't look twice at a prick of a second hand car dealer."

I turn my face so it's closer to him. It's only bravado and all I want him to do is look directly at me. It works and he stares at me menacingly. I hold his stare and move my left arm slightly towards Sinead and open my palm towards her, hoping that she sees the tent number. I break the stare and walk away without saying anything.

"Oh that was brave of him wasn't it darling, he can't be that keen on you," Richard says as I walk away.

Night...

There's no way on this Earth that Sinead is married to that pig. I keep repeating the thought, trying to convince myself it's true. But if she isn't, what the hell is this charade all about? A minute later and I come to a different conclusion. I've just been warned off by a husband who fears he's been cuckolded or is about to be. Maybe Sinead is flirty and flighty, perhaps she's offered massages to others before and they've become more than massages. No, that's bollocks - it has to be.

The tent zips begin to move slowly and they're hardly open before Sinead crawls in, moving herself along with her elbows like a soldier approaching the enemy. She gets her whole body in and sits up. She looks exhausted.

"Shit, that was hard work. Have you tried crawling on your stomach for a hundred yards in the dark, trying not to get entangled in tent ropes?" she says.

"Why the hell did you crawl here?" I ask, but she doesn't answer.

"We need to talk," she says.

Christ, that was a mother of an understatement.

She continues, "Actually I need to talk and you need to listen."

I nod.

"Right. First, Richard is not my husband..."

I try and butt in, but she tells me to be quiet and listen.

"I can't tell you who he is, but I'm not married. I was, but that was a long time ago."

Something seems to flash across her mind. "I'm assuming you're not married?"

I shake my head.

"That's what I thought. I don't know why, you just didn't seem married. So when all of this is over, we can see each other if that's what you want."

Another nod and I try again to ask questions. She puts her finger to my lips and I kiss it. She smiles and I feel like a teenager who's out on his first date.

"But until the ride's over, we can't see another. Richard's a nasty bit of work and there's a lot at stake for him, so he won't take kindly to any interference. I know I'm talking in riddles, but it's for the best. I just want to get this ride over and if you know any more, it'll all become complicated."

Sinead pauses, allowing me time to get in a question. "Has this got something to do with the Trans-Global bike team?"

Her expression changes. "Why do you think that?"

"Because I saw you and him coming out of their motorhome."

"Christ, you have been spying on me and that's what frightens me. You can't do it."

She's getting angry and I take hold of her hands, rubbing her fingers."

"Look, you've got to stop getting cross with me just because I'm worried about you."

"I'm not cross with you," she replies, "I'm worried - about you, about me."

There's the sound of a nearby tent being unzipped and Sinead jumps.

"Look I must go, if he finds the tent empty, it'll take some explaining."

It's her turn to take hold of my hands.

She continues, "So we can't meet or talk again. You've got to make him think that he's frightened you off. I told him that I was just doing you a favour by sorting out your knee, but you came on to me. He thinks I'm not interested in you."

"How did he find out about me going to your tent?"

"He's paying a couple of the security guards to keep an eye on me. He told them he suspected I was having an affair with another rider. They saw us this afternoon and rang him. That's why I had to crawl here; otherwise they might have seen me."

"Do you have to go?" I ask. "My knee is really hurting."

She kisses me. A soft lip kiss, a kiss that says 'another time'.

As she gets ready to crawl out she says, "The woman you're riding with, I've got nothing to worry about, have I?"

"No, she's my mother and she's already accounted for," I reply.

Sinead shakes her head. "I've no idea what you're talking about - have a good ride, see you at Land's End."

She pulls herself through the tent flap and disappears.

Day Five

Morning....

Perhaps I shouldn't be surprised that I slept so well. To get off to sleep I blocked out the negatives surrounding Sinead and concentrated on the positives. It wasn't difficult. I remembered her eyes, her smile, me stroking her leg, her massage, our embrace, kissing her fingers, kissing her lips.....Sleep came too easily and prematurely erased the memories.

There's ten minutes before the wake up music and all I can think of this morning are the negatives. Richard is a nasty piece of work, yet he's got some kind of hold over Sinead and it's something she can't or won't break away from. Can't means he's controlling her somehow, but what's stopping her just walking away? If she were outside my tent now and said she wanted to leave, I'd be packed in ten minutes. But she's not and it must be because she won't.

The wake up music. *'What's the story, Morning Glory?'* I've got absolutely no idea.

I'm getting better at finding my bike in the compound. It's quite simple really - it will be where I left it the night before. There are security guards at the exit each morning who are supposed to check that the number on your bike corresponds with the number on your name tag.

For the first couple of mornings they did this methodically, but then no doubt realised that it would take a very serious bike thief to get up at that time in the morning, put on full cycling kit and walk out with a bike. Even if one of the riders took a fancy to somebody else's bike, they would ride it for one day and then have to return it to the same place they stole it from, albeit it had moved about a hundred miles in the meantime.

As I'm walking towards the exit, the security guard is looking at each bike number, but letting people pass unchallenged. The guard reads my number and steps across in front of me. He's built like the proverbial shit-house door and his head is stuck onto his shoulders with no discernable neck connecting the two. People behind stop, but he waves them through. He asks to see my name tag which is around my neck and tucked inside my jersey. When I get it out, he grabs it and pulls it towards him, jerking my neck and forcing me to bend forward.

"Mark Anthony," he says, "I've been hearing a few stories about you. So if you want to enjoy the rest of your ride, I suggest you be a good boy and stop trying it on with other men's wives."

There has to be quick and appropriate response to this monkey, but I can't think of it and don't reply.

He tosses the tag towards me. "Have a good day."

Gillian was one of the riders who'd passed by and is waiting for me.

"What on earth was that all about? He looked a bit aggressive."

"Mistaken identity," I reply. "He got me confused with somebody who'd caused a bit of trouble."

"Trouble, what sort of trouble?"

"No idea," I say and walk towards the start line, hoping that the conversation is over.

Lawrence is already waiting for us at the starting line. The medics have re-dressed his arm and thigh and although everything is still a bit stiff, he says he'll be okay. I hope okay means he'll stay riding with us. Bobby Big Bollocks isn't here yet and Gillian moves off towards the start. I begin to go with her, but Lawrence questions if we should wait for Bob. I convince him that Bob might have already gone or will catch us up. I feel a bit bad, but it's not me that has to endure his company for mile after mile.

As we cross the start line, I do some simple calculations. We've crossed the start line five times and have only got to cross it four more times. I've slept in a tent for five nights and have to endure it for only four more nights. Sometime today we will have ridden for more than four and a half days and from then, will have less riding to do than we've already done. I know that this is the same as saying we're reaching half way, but that in a way is depressing. It's like saying, *'we're only halfway through'*. I much prefer, *'we've broken the back of it'*.

Sinead's treatment, rest and painkillers have improved my knee and the searing pain has been replaced by mild discomfort. I'm hoping it will stay like that for the rest of morning, which is when we take on the Kirkstone Pass, the steepest climb of the ride so far. Even before we get there, we have a long steady ascent from Carlisle into the Lake District. After the Kirkstone Pass there's a long steep descent into Windermere and then sixty or so easier miles, skirting Lancaster, through Preston and on to the base camp outside exotic Wigan. Wigan apparently has got a pier, which is pretty cool bearing in mind it's about thirty miles from the sea - it must be a long one!

After five miles, Bob joins us, huffing and puffing from the exertion of caching us up. As he latches onto Gillian, he casts me a malevolent glance. I think he believes that leaving him was all a devilish plot by me to steal the affections of Gillian.

I think of Mike as we ride along the edge of the Cumbrian Mountains which form the backbone of the Lake District. The sun and moving clouds create shapes and patterns which reflect off the slopes of the mountains to our right. Occasionally we are forced to stop for wild ponies that stand stubbornly in the middle of the road. Mike had told me on the coach from Inverness that one reason he wanted to do the ride was so that he could take photographs of the scenery. Now and again riders do stop to take photos, but most just plough on. I'd have booked a coach trip if I'd wanted to take photographs and no doubt Mike wishes that he'd done just that. I must ring him tonight.

The first pit stop is at the end of Ullswater in the shadow of Helvellyn and at the foot of the Kirkstone Pass. As we ride in, the early riders are leaving and turning right towards the foot of the pass. They're a mixture of the fast club and elite cyclists and the slowest riders who start early. The club and elite groups smile, chat and bob on and off their saddles, clearly relishing the challenge ahead. The others are silent and look petrified.

At the stop it's impossible to get away from talk about the pass. It becomes boring and depressing and I just want to get it over with. I attempted a similar climb in the Peak District during my training and failed miserably. It was a twisting pass between high walls of rock and I was doing okay until I went round a sharp bend and was hit by a strong headwind. My legs stopped turning and I couldn't clip out of the pedals in time so toppled over sideways. I then faced the problem of starting off again on a steep gradient and no matter how many times I tried, I couldn't get going and was forced to walk up. I've looked at the Kirkstone Pass on a map and it looks pretty straight and I'm hoping that I can get into some kind of a rhythm that will drag me to the top.

Three quarters of the way to the top and I'm doing alright. Some people have been forced to walk, but my legs are still turning and I'm controlling and timing my breathing with each downward push of the pedals.

The little white scorpion passes and then slows down so that after a bit, I drag myself alongside.

"How's the knee?" Sinead asks.

Surely she can't expect to have a conversation? My lungs require every millilitre of air for the blood pumping to my legs and there's no surplus for talking. I nod and make an attempt to mouth 'alright'.

"Good," she replies, "not far to go."

The scorpion gets up off the saddle, makes a quick wiggle and shoots off up the pass.

I make it to the top. A lot of people have stopped to recover and I see Lawrence looking totally fresh and smiling. I'm expecting to see Bob, but he's not there. We all started together and I'd assumed that he was in front. I look back towards the summit and see him just cycling over. I know this isn't supposed to be competitive...but! Five minutes later Gillian joins us. She's had to stop twice, but managed to get moving again and hasn't walked. This does deserve a photo and we all pose, swap cameras and then pose again.

Now I like speed, but prefer it combined with some semblance of control. The twisting descent has speed, but those four small rubber brake pads struggle to provide control. The technique is similar to driving a race car around a track, pick your braking point, brake, pick you line and power round the corner. I manage three out of the four, but struggle with one. No matter how hard I pull the brake levers, I'm always going into the bends too fast. In a car the result is called understeer, on a bike it's called '*Shit, I'm going to fall off the edge of the road*' or '*Shit, I'm going to hit that car coming the other way before I fall off the edge of the road*'. The only thing I can do is keep braking around the corner. Well not the only thing - I pray as well.

We wait at the bottom for Gillian. We're all silent, anticipating the worst. We don't have to wait too long before she comes to a stop beside us. Her face is red and she's grinning from ear to ear.

"God, I really enjoyed that," she shouts.

I'm not sure whether she's just blasphemed or was talking to her husband's boss.

We drop down to the edge of Lake Windermere, past the shores of Bowness and then head south east to skirt around Morecambe

Bay. The scenery and excitement is over for the day and we settle into an easy pace to grind out the miles until the next pit stop.

Lawrence and I ride side by side wherever we can. I ask him light-heartedly how his charts are going and fear that he may be a bit defensive. I'm wrong and he tells me how for the last couple of days, they've been very simple and uncomplicated. Without prompting, he admits that his cycling has become too competitive and about how he used to be happy to ride at a reasonable pace. He blames his marriage break-up for the anger and frustration that led him to train harder and harder. He said that the physical pain helped to numb his emotions.

For a few miles I manage to prise Bob and Gillian apart. I can sense that she's not happy and that it's got nothing to do with traffic or tiredness.

Lawrence and I ride together again.

"I know what I meant to tell you," he says. "I found out something about the blond girl Sinead and her mysterious husband."

I try to act only partially interested, but gently press him.

He continues. "Well it might only be tittle-tattle, but they're tied in with Trans-Global somehow. Apparently Trans-Global are trying out a prototype bike made in China which they want to use in the Tour de France next month."

I'm getting impatient. "But what's that got to do with the girl and her husband?"

"The rumour is that her husband is representing the Chinese manufacturer and will be the sole UK and European importer. You can imagine how keen he'll be that the bikes are launched on the back of being used on the Tour by a big new team."

"So why all the secrecy?"

"Two reasons. Firstly it's a bit like new cars; they'll want to keep it under wraps and go into the market with a big splash and wrong foot other manufacturers. Secondly, Haskins proudly claim that the ride is strictly for charitable purposes and isn't used for commercial activities. "

"And the girl, where's does she fit in?" I ask.

"Her full name is Sinead O'Connor and some of the guys know her from a few years ago when she was a professional in Ireland. They think she might be testing a cheaper road bike."

"Who's '*they*', where did you get all this from?"

"I was sitting with some of the elite and club riders at dinner last night and they were talking about it. They like nothing better than a good gossip, so it might not be totally right, but it seems to make sense. Her husband is also using Sinead for publicity material. Someone spotted a photographer taking pictures of her on the bike, but they make sure that they remove the entrant number and anything else that could link the photo to the ride. I'm looking forward to seeing the pictures. She has got a nice bum."

"Has she? I hadn't noticed." I reply.

Afternoon....

The second pit stop is at a sprawling country pub and we use the garden to eat and drink. I notice that Gillian isn't sitting with us and assume that she's gone to the toilet. She must find it frustrating when we disappear behind a tree every so often whilst she's forced to wait for the stops. I decide to use the pub's toilet before we set off again and follow the signs to the back of the building. Gillian is sitting on a low wall and I sit down beside her.

"Are you okay?" I ask.

"No I'm bloody not!" she replies. "I really don't think I can take any more, the man's like a bloody leech. I'm serious, I can't face another four days of it. The cycling's hard enough and I need my own space. He's suffocating me."

I've never seen her so agitated and she continues. "He's one of those men that women have a sixth sense about; the ones that touch you for no reason and when they do, it makes your skin creep. The best way to deal with them is to avoid them, but I can't do that, I can't get away.

"So what's wrong with my original idea?" I ask.

"To tell him to piss off? You might be right, but it's not in my nature. And I would feel guilty, I'm sure a bit of it might be because he genuinely wants to help me."

Gillian looks down at her chest. "These don't help either, but I can't do anything about them, that's just the way they are and cycling makes them worse."

All I can do is smile. Her candidness takes me aback.

She continues unabashed. "My husband says they are a gift from God and that I shouldn't hide my light under a bushel." She laughs. "We do have a bit of fun with them."

"Gillian. Stop there. Too much information!" I say.

She laughs again. "No, I mean we find it interesting to see how people react to a vicar's wife with... well, you know what I mean."

I nod.

"In fact, I find them a very good way to judge men," she says. "There are three types. The men who become fixated and can't raise their eyes and the ones who purposefully look straight at my face, but take a quick peek when they think I'm not looking. Bob definitely is the first type, whereas you are a gentleman and fall into the second. "

"So what about the third group? You said there were three groups."

"Ah yes, I've no time for them, they're the ones who don't look at all."

Gillian laughs loudly and I suspect that it's a little party piece of hers.

It's time for us to make a move and I get up. I don't want to say anything, but feel compelled.

"If you like, I'll have a quiet word with Bob and see if I can get him to back off a bit."

Gillian grabs my arm. "Oh would you? I really would be grateful."

I have absolutely no idea how I'm going to do it, or what I'm going to say. Perhaps I'll just tell him to piss off.

The last stage of the day's ride is memorable for being totally unmemorable. The only bit to break the tedium is the ride through the centre of Preston, which Gillian takes in her stride given that the traffic is quite light. The base camp is a little bit north of Wigan so we are denied the pleasure of experiencing its delights first hand. I don't see any sign of a pier.

I decide against a cup of tea in case Sinead is in the food tent and I arouse the interest of a certain security guard. I get to the front of the queue for the tent number allocation and as normal, the girl gives me the number and writes it on my hand.

I'm about to walk away when she says, "Mr Anthony, do you think you could go and see Seb in the admin office before you go to your tent?"

I ask her why and she says she has no idea.

The admin office is a screened off section of the food tent. There are a couple of trestle tables with computers on them and various boxes of files. There is a man of around thirty five and a younger girl sitting in front of the computers.

I walk in. "I been asked to see somebody called Seb. My name's Mark Anthony," I say.

The man holds out his hand. "Yes, thank you Mr. Anthony, I'm Seb." He turns to the girl. "Sarah, do you think you could give Mr. Anthony and I a few minutes?"

The girl doesn't reply, but gets up and leaves us alone. The man gestures for me to sit on a wooden garden chair and pulls up another one so he's sitting opposite me.

"These things are always a bit awkward," he says. "You've paid a lot of money to take part in the Haskin Long Britain Ride, and we want everyone to enjoy the experience, but unfortunately there are occasions when somebody's behaviour affects our other riders, and we need to have a word with them."

I'm tired, sweaty and hungry and the last thing I need is this sanctimonious prat talking to me like I'm a naughty schoolboy.

"Seb, sorry I didn't catch your surname. Cut the crap and just tell me what I'm supposed to have done."

"Johnston, Seb Johnston. We've had a complaint that you've been harassing one of the lady riders."

"So, this lady has made a complaint?"

"No, her husband."

"Her husband's a rider is he? What's his name?"

Johnston's beginning to look a bit flustered, I don't think he expected the schoolboy to fight back.

"No, he's not a rider, he's supporting his wife who happens to be an elite rider."

"So what's this man's name then, what's his wife's name? I think I have the right to know who's made this complaint."

Johnston hesitates. "His name is Richard Seymour and his wife's name is Sinead O'Connor - she uses her maiden name."

I'm determined to use this opportunity to find out as much as I can about Mr Richard Seymour, even if it means flying a few kites.

"But she's not an elite rider is she? She doesn't wear the Haskin kit and she wasn't part of the presentation on the first night."

Johnston's been sucked into defending his position. "No, strictly speaking she's not an elite rider, but she's a well respected ex-professional rider, who asked to join the ride as preparation for returning to national events. Her husband is here to provide support."

"So why are you taking his word that I harassed his wife?"

I've pushed as far as I can go.

"I've no reason to doubt him and he says that a security guard witnessed you being asked by Miss O'Connor to leave her tent, and that she was very distressed. Apparently she offered to get you some pain relieving gel and you followed her into her tent."

"That Mr. Johnston, is a load of bollocks. If I was in the tent how could the security guard see me being asked to leave?"

He ignores my question, picks up a plastic wallet and pulls out a familiar piece of paper. He studies it silently for a few seconds.

"Mr. Seymour said you were a second hand car dealer."

"Yes, that right, but what's that got to with anything?"

"It says on your application form that you're a company director."

Jesus! This guy is a tosser and has just opened the door for me to play my ace.

"I am. I'm managing director of M.A. Motorsports who are amongst other things, second hand car dealers. Dealers in very expensive second hand cars. Have you heard of Sir Peter Jeffries? He's a non-executive board member of Haskin."

Johnston doesn't reply so I continue. "Well of course you've heard of him, he's a very influential man and also a client of mine. I managed to find him an extremely rare aluminium bodied E Type racer for which he was extremely grateful. In fact, we're sharing the driving at an event at Goodwood in September. Actually it was him who first suggested that I do this ride; he's very keen on getting feedback on how well it's all gone.

I remember something else. "He sent me a text wishing me good luck - would you like to see it?"

I delve in my jersey pocket to get out my phone.

Don't you just love it when things go right. And every word is true. No second hand car dealer exaggerations at all. I find the text and hold my phone in front of him. He appears to lose his confidence.

"So Mr. Johnston," I say, "you have Mr. Seymour's story and you have my response that his accusation is a load of bollocks. Now if you'll excuse me, I need a shower."

As I turn my back on him, I allow myself to bend my elbow and raise my arm with a clenched fist and utter *'Yeeees'* under my breath.

Evening....

I'm in the massage and physio queue which is a little bit shorter than last night and remember that I need to ring Mike. He's pleased to hear from me and I give him a potted resume of the last couple of days. I ask him to do me another favour and go on the Internet to see if he can find any information on a Richard Seymour who has some connection with bike imports. I tell him I'll ring him back later.

The physio does the same thing to my leg as Sinead and it hurts like hell again. Unfortunately there's no back massage this time and no temptation to stroke the thigh of a seventeen stone Brummie with a shaven head.

Where's the bloody time gone? It's quarter to ten and I've only just finished my dinner. I haven't spoken to Bob about Gillian and I've still got to ring Mike back. I go into the chill-out tent to look for Bob, but he's not there. Lawrence is at the bar. It seems that he's well and truly broken his pledge of abstinence. Presumably a hangover has little effect when he rides at our pace. He calls me over and I accept his offer of a drink.

Lawrence is the sort of chap that knows everything about everything, so without being specific, I mention that I met one of Haskin's organisers, a guy called Seb Johnston.

Lawrence immediately corrects me.

"I can see that you've got a lot to learn about corporate fund raising," he says. "It's like a layer cake, with the base layer being the deserving charity. Think of all the money that you, me and everybody else has paid to enter the ride as treacle that's poured onto the cake. It will slowly absorb into it, but each layer will retain a certain amount. Hopefully by the time the treacle reaches the bottom there's enough left for the charity in the base layer.

I can't help but admire Lawrence's eloquence and

analogy. The beer has obviously helped, but he's someone who is totally at home with the law and business, but a bit at sea with the world outside.

"So what are all these layers?" I ask.

"At the top are Haskins. Although they contribute a fair amount of treacle, they take a bit back by subsidising all of their own riders and using it as a means to run corporate soirees and PR events. Next down is CCF who employ Seb Johnston.

"So who or what is CCF?" I ask.

Corporate Charity Funding, they are basically brokers who put big corporates in touch with charities and agree a mutually acceptable deal. It might be a charity ball, a celebrity golf day or a bike ride. So Haskin effectively become the figurehead and CCF take it on from there.

"So CCF are Johnston's company."

"Good lord no. He's a minnow who gives the impression that he's responsible for organising everything, but of course he doesn't. That's where the next layer comes in - the sports event company. They do all the hard work and in turn, put all the other layers in place; the caterers, the transport company, the security, etcetera etcetera. It's an awful lot of layers."

It comes as relief to find out that Johnston can't take any credit for the actual organisation of the ride. This is well oiled and slickly organised event and way above the capabilities of a jumped up little prick like him. No wonder he went a bit pale when I mentioned Sir Peter Jeffries. Sir Peter has a lot of clout with Haskin and Johnston's bosses at CCF wouldn't want to lose, what is I'm sure, a very lucrative contract.

Lawrence agrees that if CCF are facilitating a large donation from Trans-Global, they're quite possibly turning a blind eye if they know that Trans-Global and Seymour are testing a new bike. I say to Lawrence that if there's a rumour about the bike testing, surely Haskins will get to hear about it. He replies that provided it remains no more than a rumour, and doesn't look like it's going to become an embarrassment, Haskin won't really be interested. He adds that they're probably touting for work from Trans-Global, or are possibly already working for them.

I need to get to bed and decide that Bob will have to wait until the morning. On my way back to the tent I ring Mike.

"No luck. I'm afraid", he says. "I can't find anything about a bike importer or anything to do with bikes under the name Richard Seymour. I've got quite a few solicitors and accountants, a hairdresser from Bootle and a surgical instrument importer from Dorking."

I thank Mike and promise I'll ring him in a few days. He says that as he's in Illfracombe, he'll drive down to meet up with us when we get into Devon. I hope he does, it will be good to see him again.

As I'm walking back to my tent, something Mike said spins around my head. The car park is behind the main tent complex and I double back and go into the food tent on the pretext of getting a cup of coffee. The tent is practically deserted and I slip through an open flap at the back. The car park is facing me and I can see the two Trans-Global motorhomes. The lights are on, but there is no sign of anybody. I spot the 4x4 which is backed up to the perimeter railing. There's just enough light to make out the sticker on the rear window. I'm right - *Supplied by Mannings of Dorking.*

Night....

As much as I want her to, Sinead doesn't crawl through my tent flap tonight. My only consolation is a melted chocolate fudge bar and salami stick that I find in my sweaty jersey pocket.

Day Six

Morning....

'Don't Stop Believin'' - this morning's wake up music. Nice sentiment, but I'm not sure what or who I believe any more. What I do believe is the discomfort as I try to move. When does discomfort become pain? I could make excuses and say that I slept awkwardly, but when you're sleeping in a sleeping bag in a cramped tent, what alternative is there to sleeping awkwardly? It's like some kind of sick joke. Let's persuade normal, everyday people into thinking that they can do something special, like cycle over a hundred miles a day for nine days and just when they believe us, we'll make them live in a crappy, tiny, sodding tent.

I've woken up in a bad mood.

My bad mood is slowing everything down. Packing my bag is a disaster and like the first day my stuff is spilling out, but this time, no matter how hard I try, I can't do the zip up. So I tip the whole lot out and start again. I'm going to be late getting to breakfast and I've still got to talk to Bob about Gillian. It would be so easy to say to her that I didn't get the chance and hope that the problem goes away, but I know it won't. She was pretty wound up and upset yesterday afternoon and she's the sort to quietly give up and slip away without wanting to make a fuss.

Bob is in the food tent having breakfast and shouting at some people who've been unfortunate enough to end up on his table. I try to catch his eye, hoping that I can beckon him outside for a chat, but he either doesn't notice me or doesn't want to. He's just finishing his breakfast and if I join the queue for food, by the time I get back he'll probably have left.

There's a vacant chair next to him and I sit down. He ignores me and keeps on shouting so I tap him on the shoulder.

"Bob, Gillian's asked if I would have a word with you."

I know it's not strictly true, but it sounds better than me wanting a word with him.

Gillian's name grabs his attention. "What sort of word?" he shouts.

A few people on the table look at us.

"I think it would be better if we spoke outside," I say.

Bob leans back on his chair and shouts. "Better if we speak outside?"

He's now guaranteed the attention of the whole table.

Sod it! If you want to be an arsehole, so be it.

"Gillian would prefer it if you paid her a little less attention," I say loudly.

Bob hesitates for a second. "Gillian would prefer it if I paid her a little less attention?"

"Yes, you're crowding her. She just needs a bit of space."

"She just needs a bit of space?"

I snap. I'm hungry, tired and don't want to be having this conversation.

"Bob, will you stop repeating everything I say. You sound like a bloody parrot. Please listen. Gillian is a lovely woman who's struggling at the moment and all I'm asking is that you pay her a little less attention."

"A little less attention?" I can't believe he's done it again, but Bob then adds something original. He really is shouting now and it's not just our table who can hear.

"I get it. You want me to back off so you can get in there. You've made that pretty obvious from the start. Trying to ride between us whenever you can and riding off with her yesterday morning. Leaving me behind. What's the matter? Has it really got to you because she prefers my company to yours?"

"Whatever."

I sound like a morose teenage girl, but I'm drained of energy and get up. With half the food tent staring at me, breakfast is out of the question. As I walk out of the food tent Seb Johnston is standing in the doorway of the admin office. It's not far from where Bob and I were sitting and no doubt Johnston heard some or a lot of our conversation. I look away as I go past.

By the time I get to the start queue, Gillian and Lawrence are already waiting. I'm not sure if they were in the food tent when it kicked off with Bob, but we exchange normal pleasantries and nothing is said. Gillian probably won't ask, so I tell her that I've had a chat with Bob, but leave out the details. I say that it didn't go well and that I have no idea if it will make any difference or not. She thanks me profusely and crosses her fingers. I cross mine in return.

My mind's stewing over the row with Bob. It didn't need to be a row - it could have been a sensible conversation between two adults. It wasn't as if I was accusing him of anything. After riding for a couple of miles I feel a compulsion to ride alone and fast in order to flush out my anger. The three of us are waiting behind a van at traffic lights and I squeeze up the side of it so that I'm at the front. As the lights change I get out of the saddle and sprint off. For the first mile or two, I ride as fast as I can, my lungs struggling for air and my legs screaming. I then settle down to what I consider is a fast pace. With ninety miles still to go, it's probably suicide, but I don't care. Just as I'm thinking that I'm doing reasonably well, Lawrence cruises up alongside as if he's on a Sunday morning ride.

"You might have said that you wanted to stretch your legs today, I wouldn't have had that extra pint last night."

Stretch my legs? They feel that they've been on a mediaeval rack!

"I'm sorry," I reply, "I just felt the need to be on my own for a bit. Is Gillian all right?"

"I'm not sure," Lawrence answers. "Bob caught us up and they're together as usual. I don't know what you think, but I get the impression that she really doesn't like him."

I tell him about my chat with Gillian yesterday afternoon and my altercation with Bob this morning. I'm surprised by his response.

"It's a pity your talk with him doesn't seem to have worked. He's really getting on my nerves as well. He thinks he knows such a lot about cycling, well, he thinks he knows a lot about everything, but most of it's either bullshit or total rubbish."

"Lawrence," I say, "can you do me a favour? Could you drop back and try and help Gillian get away from him. There's no way I can do it."

Lawrence nods. "No problem. See you at the first stop."

It begins to rain. I've already got my waterproof on, but this isn't just rain, it's a deluge and the open Cheshire country road provides no opportunity to shelter. I'm getting very wet and cold and beginning feel the effect of not having had breakfast. We turn onto a main road somewhere near Knutsford and pass a petrol station where I stop and take refuge under the canopy. Through the rain, like a mirage in the desert, I can see a Little Chef in the adjacent car park.

I expect it to be packed with soaked cyclists, but there aren't any. It feels strange. I'm back in the real world for the first time in six days.

It had to be done! I'm waiting for my Olympic Breakfast to be cooked whilst drinking a large mug of coffee. The rain's still coming down in sheets and I watch out of the window as rider after rider ploughs on, seemingly oblivious to the oasis they are passing on their left hand side. As the waitress fills my mug up with more coffee and serves my breakfast, I see Gillian and Lawrence ride past. Although it's a bit difficult to see through the rain splattered window, I can't see Bobby Big Bollocks.

I get up to pay the bill, but the waitress says that it's on the house and tells me to put it towards my charity. I should be honest and tell her I don't have a charity. I'd decided that I'd paid Haskin enough money to take part and that some of that money would filter down to their much vaunted good causes. I also didn't want to be one of those people who pester you for sponsorship and you're left with the impression that you're paying for them to go off and have a good time. Not that I'd call this having a good time.

By the time I get to the first stop it's no longer raining, the warm wind has partially dried my clothes and although the Olympic Breakfast is lying a bit heavily on my stomach, I'm feeling better.

Gillian and Lawrence are about to leave as I ride in. There's no sign of Bobby Big whatsits and I stop alongside them. Gillian is beaming and I don't need to ask why.

"He's gone and I don't think he'll be back," she says.

"But Lawrence said he was riding with you."

"He was. He told me that you'd asked him to stay away because you were jealous of the relationship that had developed between him and me."

"So what did you say?"

Gillian smiles. "I told him to piss off."

I recognise the girl behind the timing system laptop and tell Gillian and Lawrence to ride on and that I'll try and catch them up after I've had a pee and a drink.

"Soon the good, the bad and ugly will ride again," says Lawrence.

My God! Lawrence has made a joke - well sort of. Gillian and I laugh politely and resist the temptation to ask him for a fuller explanation.

"Hi, another exciting day at the office," I say to the girl with the laptop.

She laughs. "Do you want to know how your girlfriend is doing today?"

"She'd not my girlfriend," I reply.

"Ah, but you'd like her to be. She's very pretty."

134

"I have absolutely no idea what you're talking about," I say smiling and she returns the smile.

"What's her number?"

My mind goes blank.

"What's her name?"

"O'Connor, Sinead O'Connor." It still sounds funny when I say it.

The girl scrolls through a few screens. "Well you're out of luck, the elite and fast club riders are doing the Long Mynd loop and they've already been through. You might catch them up if you hurry. You can borrow my car!"

The Long Mynd loop adds another fifteen miles and includes a one-in-four gradient climb on a single track, badly made up road. It was never going to be an option for me, but probably was for Lawrence.

I quickly catch up Lawrence and Gillian. The Olympic Breakfast must have finally lit a fire inside me and my knee doesn't feel too bad.

Riding alongside Lawrence, I say, "Lawrence, if you want to go on and have a shot at Long Mynd, I'll keep Gillian company now."

Lawrence smiles. "Do you know that one of the reasons I entered this ride was because of Long Mynd. I really wanted the chance to go up it with top cyclists so I could see how I compare, but now, I couldn't give a toss. I'd rather just tootle along with you two."

I could take offence at having my cycling prowess described as *'tootling'*, but I don't. I was wrong about Lawrence. He's a really nice chap.

Afternoon...

Ignoring the masochistic detour over Long Mynd, this is the easiest day so far and apart from the occasional short climb, the roads have been mercifully flat. Since the second stop we've made good time and are moving along easily.

The three of us are cycling through a small village when Lawrence shouts for us to stop. We pull up outside a sign which says *'Cream Teas'*.

Lawrence says, "Right, we are now going to experience what riding in the English countryside is all about. I'm going to treat us all to a cream tea."

For the second time in one day, I return to the real world, although I'm not sure whether sitting in a perfect English garden with the sun shining and eating warm scones with jam and clotted cream, can accurately be called the real world.

Lawrence insists on paying and we get back on our bikes. There's only fifteen miles to go on fairly easy roads and we'll be back at the base camp by four thirty. The tribulation of this morning seems a long time ago.

I'm in the queue to get my tent number and looking forward to my Posh Wash and a little nap before dinner. I get to the desk and give the girl my name and she nervously glances at the other girl sitting next to her.

"Mr Anthony," she says. "Do you think you could go to the admin office please?"

Christ! It's déjà vu.

"Why?" I ask, although I know she won't tell me.

"I'm afraid I don't know."

"What about my tent number?"

"They'll deal with that," she replies.

There are two people in the admin office. Seb Johnston and the security guard without a neck who stopped me yesterday morning. I get the feeling that they've been waiting for me. On the floor in front of the security guard is my bag.

"Mr Anthony, we meet again," Johnston says.

"What's this all about?"

"It's about you Mr Anthony. About you leaving the ride."

"You are joking aren't you? I thought we went through all that yesterday."

"Yes well," Johnston says, "that was before you decided to have a row with a Haskin partner in front of everybody in a crowded food tent. I'm afraid in light of that, and yesterday's complaint, I have no alternative other than to ask you to leave the ride."

"You can ask all you fucking like, I'm not going anywhere."

The security guard edges forward slightly.

"I'm afraid that if you read the terms and conditions of entry, we are quite within our rights, so please don't make things difficult. There really is no point," Johnston says.

"So did the Haskin's partner tell you what the row was all about?"

Johnston nods towards the security guard who picks up my bag.

"I'm sorry, I'm not prepared to discuss the details. Now Steve here will drive you to Ludlow Station. You should be able to get home tonight."

"What about a shower? I haven't had a shower and I'm still in cycling clothes. What about my bike?"

I think I detect a sly smile on Johnston's face as he replies. "Well you could have a shower, but Steve would need to stay with you. I'm sure you can change in the toilets at the train station. As for the bike, that will be returned as the original arrangements and left at the drop-off point a week after the ride finishes."

I remember Peter Jeffries. "I just need to make a telephone call," I say.

Johnston does smile this time. "Haskin have tried to contact Sir Peter Jeffries, but he's out of the country and his office could not confirm that you are known to him. But feel free to try and speak to him."

I get out my phone and look up the number. I have two. One is his personal mobile that he uses when he's not working and the other is the number of Stella, his PA. Shit! Both numbers go through to voicemail. I leave messages for them to ring me back.

Christ! This is a nightmare. Somebody must be able to help - Lawrence, he's a lawyer.

"I need to speak to a friend I'm riding with," I say.

"I'm sorry that won't be possible. Now if you don't mind, Steve will take you to the station. If you leave it any longer you won't get home tonight and we wouldn't want you sleeping on the platform would we?"

The guard sniggers, moves forward and grabs my arm pulling me towards the door. I shake him off.

"All right, all right. Get your hands off me - I'm going."

Johnston has the last word. "Steve, take him through the back. Mr Anthony has already caused enough scenes."

The guard guides me through a flap in the tent which leads directly to the car park. I can see the black 4x4 parked alongside the Trans-Global motorhomes and hope I get a last look at Sinead, but there's no sign of life. I'm bundled into the back seat of a car and my bag is thrown into the boot.

I've no idea how far it is to Ludlow, but guess it can't be too far, maybe fifteen or twenty minutes.

As soon as we drive off, No-Neck Steve starts talking.

"Bugger me, you know 'ow to pick 'em don't you. Still I can see the attraction of the girl - she's fit. Can't see how she's with that crook, money I suppose. And then you pick a fuckin' fight with a Haskin partner. You've got a death wish son."

I don't want to talk but...

"Why do you call him a crook?" I ask.

No-Neck Steve looks around and smiles. I wish he'd keep his eyes on the road.

"'Cos there's not much difference between us security guards and crooks. Most of us have been on both sides, so we can smell 'em. It's not just me, a lot of the boys thought it. He's a nasty bit of work. Comes across all posh, but their sort, they're usually the real article."

"I heard he was involved in providing bikes to the Russians."

He snorts. "Yes, we 'eard that one as well. If he runs a fuckin' bike shop, then I'm Mickey Mouse. That story's a fairytale - a smokescreen. No, he's into something dodgy."

"Like what?"

"You can never tell with the Russkies and their sort. Money launderin', arms, drugs, prossies - could be anything.

We're on the outskirts of Ludlow and picking up signs for the station.

Evening....

I've just missed a train. No-Neck Steve stood over me whilst I bought my ticket and we're now sitting on the platform.

"Look, there's fifty minutes until the next train, surely you're not going to wait?" I say.

"I'm s'posed to make sure you get on the train," he replies.

"Oh and what am I going to do now? I've got my ticket and there's only one place I can go and that's home. I need to get out of these sweaty clothes, so are you going to wait outside the toilet for me? You'll get arrested."

No-Neck Steve smiles. "You might 'ave a point. It's s'posed to be my night off and me and the motorbike boys are going out for few beers, so I wouldn't mind shootin' off."

Surprisingly, he holds out his hand. "I'ope you get 'ome all right mate. You were well and truly done up - just like a fuckin' kipper."

I watch him drive away and then go out to the taxi rank at the front of the station. There's a solitary taxi waiting and I ask the driver if he can take me to a bed and breakfast.

Night....

My room seems enormous although it can only be ten feet by eight. The ceiling seems suspended in the sky somewhere. The bed is soft and I can move without restriction. I'm well and truly back in the real world, but I shouldn't be here. I should be in my tiny tent; hemmed into my sleeping bag, struggling to find a comfortable position and listening to the coughs, snores and farts of my fellow campers. I should be counting down the days and miles and with three more days to go, feeling for the first time, reasonably confident that I'm going to finish.

All those months of training and preparation are well and truly down the drain. I go over and over the fifteen minutes in the admin tent when it all ended. I must have been able to do more - I should have done more. It feels now that I just curled up and let them throw me out.

I'm also hungry, very hungry. Our cream tea was eight hours ago and I haven't eaten since. I can't risk going into the town to eat for fear of meeting No-Neck Steve and his mates or anybody else to do with the ride.

I'm not sure why I didn't just wait for the train and put the whole bloody fiasco behind me. Maybe I'll wake up tomorrow and decide to do just that.

I need a piece of paper and a pen to draw a Lawrence-type diagram of the last six days. Six days? It feels like six months.

If I were to draw a diagram, Sinead would be in the centre. If it weren't for her I wouldn't be here now. The spat with Bob was just manna from heaven for Johnston and Seymour to get me thrown out. But what do I know about Sinead? Mike's Internet search confirmed that Sinead O'Connor is her real name and she's too good a rider to be an impersonator. Anyway, Lawrence said that some of the elite riders knew her. There's no way that she's married to Seymour. She said she's not, and every instinct tells me that it's true. She said that she'd been married before which tied in with what Mike's told me. I think through each encounter with her and remember something. When she was sorting out my knee in the tent, she said that she was a nurse, but was it just a joke? She certainly knew what she was doing, but she could easily have learnt that when she was cycling professionally. Anyway, it was more physio than nursing.

So where does Richard Seymour fit on my chart? Alongside Sinead, but there's no thick line connecting them. He certainly isn't her loving husband who's come along to give her encouragement and TLC as suggested by Johnston. Lawrence's story about him being involved in bike importing all seemed to fit until No-Neck Steve dismissed it as a smokescreen for something more sinister. So what about Steve's suspicions? They could be no more than that; the imaginings of a bunch of bored security guards. I try and think logically. Whatever Seymour's involvement with the Trans-Global team, it has to be connected to cycling. Why go to these lengths if it wasn't? I can remember only one other small thing. The coincidence that there's a Richard Seymour in Dorking who imports surgical instruments and the Dorking garage sticker on the back of the 4x4. But that's probably all it is, a coincidence.

There's definitely a very thick line that links Seb Johnston to Seymour and Trans-Global. I'm in this B&B because Richard Seymour pulled Johnston's strings. That's probably nothing more than money talking. Trans-Global have made a large donation to join the ride which means that CCF get a cut and Johnston will do anything to please them.

I wonder if Haskin need to be included on the chart. Johnston might well have been bluffing when he said Haskin had spoken to Peter Jeffries, but it would have been an easy bluff to call had Peter answered his phone. So the likelihood is that someone from Haskin did call him, but God knows what crap Haskin were fed by Johnston. I can't be bothered to consider Bob. Yes, he's from Haskin, but is just an irritating, insignificant little wart who unwittingly provided the ammunition to have me shot. No, I think that Haskin are blissfully unaware that their worthy event is being manipulated by others.

That just leaves Gillian and Lawrence. There's no need to include them in the chart, they really are innocents. I wonder if they realise I've gone. We had no rules for meeting up after the day's ride, but usually bumped into one another during the evening. The fact that we haven't probably won't register and they'll only miss me when I'm not at the morning start.

I think about ringing Mike and unburdening on him, but decide against it. It will take some explaining and I haven't got the energy tonight. I'll ring him tomorrow.

I scroll through stuff on my phone. In received calls there's a number I don't recognise, but, I work out that it's when Gillian rang me about Mike. She goes to sleep early so I can't ring her now, but it's good that I'll be able to speak to her tomorrow. I go through the list of calls I've made. The ones to Mike, a couple to my parents, plus one more. I look at the date and the time and try to work out who the call was to. It was a two thirty on the Friday before we started. I remember - Inverness Airport waiting for the coach. Bob and Lawrence had gone back into the terminal for a cup of coffee and asked me to ring them if the coach turned up. It did and I rang, but I can't remember which of them gave me their number.

There's a fifty-fifty chance I'll get Lawrence. He's unlikely to be asleep yet and I press the number to redial it. The phone rings and rings and then clicks - *'This is the voicemail of Bob Casey please leave........'*

That's the way my luck's going is at the moment.

My phone rings. The number displayed is the number I've just rung. Bob is ringing back. My finger hovers over the '*decline*' button. No sod it, I fancy a word with Bobby Big Bollocks. I press the '*accept*' button.

I answer with an anonymous, "Hello."

"This is Bob Casey, I've just had a missed call from someone on your number."

"Bob, it's Mark, Mark Anthony."

"Who?"

"Mark, Gillian's friend."

The cogs whirr and the penny drops.

"Why the bloody hell are you ringing me at this time of night? I was asleep."

My anger switch is flicked.

"Well it must be nice to be able to get some sleep. I'm in a grotty B&B and can't sleep because I've been kicked off the ride thanks to you."

"What the hell are you talking about?"

He asked, so I tell him. He tries to butt in from time to time without success and my invective is relentless. There's a small pause whilst I take the opportunity to breathe.

Bob manages to speak.

"I can see that you're a little upset..." I start again....

"Shut up Mark, or I'll hang up. Do you want to hear what I've got to say?" Bob says.

Not really, but I'm silent for a second which allows him to talk.

"I can assure you that I didn't make any complaint to the organisers about you. For a start, I wouldn't have had time before we started *and* I wouldn't have done it anyway. It was a heated exchange, that's all. This ride isn't easy, we're all suffering and a bit stressed."

I make a noise down the phone that I hope sounds like some kind of apology.

Bob continues. "If what you're telling me is true and they're using my name, it's outrageous. I'll speak to them first thing tomorrow and see if I can sort it out. I'll ring you when I've spoken to them. Now if you don't mind, I really need to get some sleep."

More mumbles from me and Bob hangs up.

Of course what I glossed over in my tirade was the complaint from Seymour the previous day and I'm now trying to remember if Johnston actually said that Bob had made a complaint. I can't help feeling that when Bob speaks to Johnston there will be a different spin to the story.

Still, it does appear that I got Bob wrong - well perhaps just a tiny bit.

Day Seven

Morning...

'Homeward Bound, I wish I was homeward bound.................I'm sitting in a railway station got a ticket for my destination....'

Was it all a bad dream and I'm really in my tent listening to the wake up music? I open my eyes and the answer is no. The room seems much smaller in the morning light and the ceiling much closer. I can hear music. A radio is playing somewhere in the B&B, but the music isn't Simon and Garfunkel. Perhaps that bit was a dream.

It's just past eight o'clock and I'm glad that my body clock resisted the temptation to wake me at five thirty. The B&B lady said that they served breakfast up until eight thirty and there's no way I'm going to miss it. The scones and cream were seventeen long hours ago.

The B&B could learn a lesson about a decent shower from Posh Wash. The water is lukewarm and I need to dance around the tiny cubicle in order to get the three weak streams of water to touch my body.

As I move a pile of clothes my phone falls out. There's a text message.

'Couldn't see organisers this morning will try again tonight, Bob.'

I reply, '*Thanks if u get a chance can u tell Gillian and Lawrence what's happened Thanks Mark.*'

I can't believe that twenty four hours after our spat in the food tent, Bob and I are texting one another.

I've got a ticket for my destination, but I'm not sitting in a railway station. I'm standing outside the B&B on a deserted side street in Ludlow. I haven't got a suitcase or a guitar in my hand, just a bag of smelly cycling clothes and there's no way I'm homeward bound. Ignoring Sinead, which is something I'm finding impossible to do, I haven't invested hours of training and thousands of pounds in this ride just to walk away with my tail between my legs. I've been, for want of a better description, '*done up like an effin kipper*'. I've no real idea of what I am going to do, but I'm not going home.

I need to find somewhere to gather my thoughts and work out some kind of plan. After giving up on the bitter warm liquid that the B&B passed off as coffee, I need a decent cappuccino. The faux Italian coffee chains haven't infiltrated the depths of Shropshire, but being such a genteel town, Ludlow has no shortage of tea rooms and coffee shops.

I order a coffee and as I sit down the phone rings. It's a call from Sir Peter Jeffries's PA, Stella. I'd forgotten that I'd left her a message.

" Mark Anthony," I answer.

"Mark, it's Stella. You left me a message to ring you. What on earth is going on? Have you got yourself in some kind of trouble?"

How does she know that? Johnston obviously wasn't bluffing.

"Yes, sort of," I reply. "Is Sir Peter there? I really need to speak to him urgently."

"No, he's salmon fishing in the North of Iceland and not back until late tonight."

Great!

"Can I get hold of him?" I ask.

"No, not really. There's no signal where he's fishing. He has to drive into a town to make calls. I spoke to him last night and told him about the call from Haskin, but the line wasn't very good and I'm not sure he took it all in. He asked me to deal with it."

"Stella, can you tell me about the call from Haskin?" I ask.

In her usual meticulous manner she tells me how a partner of Haskin rang to speak with Sir Peter. When she told him that he was out of the country, he asked if Sir Peter knew me because I'd been involved in an argument on the ride and had claimed to be known to him. She'd replied that she was not at liberty to disclose information on Sir Peter's personal acquaintances and that he needed to speak with Sir Peter on Monday.

As ever, Stella's protocol is perfect, albeit not very helpful to my cause.

She insists on knowing what's happened so that she can tell Sir Peter. She really means she wants to decide if he needs to be involved at all. I try and keep the details down to a bare minimum, but it's difficult as she asks a lot of questions. You don't try and pull the wool over the eyes of the PA to an important and rich client. I concoct half a story about accidentally upsetting a Haskin partner doing the ride, who then started throwing his weight about. I didn't tell her that they'd thrown me out. I'll leave the full story until I can speak to Peter.

Whilst I was talking to Stella another call had come in and I order another cup of coffee, retrieve the call and ring back.

The questions are fired at me like a machine gun.

"Mark! Where are you? What happened? Are you all right?"

It's Gillian and it's obvious that Bob has told her. The nasty side of me thinks that he has taken great delight in telling them that I'd been thrown off the ride, but maybe that's unfair. I assure her that I'm fine, but say that I can't tell her the whole story now. They are about to leave the first pit stop somewhere near Hereford and head towards Ross on Wye and then on to Chepstow. My plan is far from complete, in fact it's not even started and I ask Gillian to ring when me they reach the second pit stop.

Ludlow is so genteel that it doesn't appear to have a second hand car dealer. I've been walking around for half an hour and haven't found so much as a small backstreet garage. I'm walking along the main street when a flatbed lorry passes with Posh Wash cabins stacked on it. It's followed by a convoy of more lorries - the base camp is on the move. I slip into a shop doorway so that I can't be seen. The organisers have duplicate base camp set-ups which have leapfrogged each other down the country and these lorries will be travelling to set up tomorrow's base camp. It really is an amazing logistical achievement. The convoy stops at traffic lights and are caught up by the Trans-Global procession of riders and support vehicles. A black 4x4 stops nearly opposite me and I can see Richard Seymour. He's looking straight ahead, but I turn my back and edge further into the doorway.

I give up looking for a car dealer and walk to the station. The taxi driver who took me to the B&B last night is waiting in the taxi rank and confirms that there is only one garage in Ludlow that sells cars. It's on the outskirts of the town and five minutes later he drops me off outside. I tell him not to wait.

An hour later, I've got the keys to an anonymous looking five year old people carrier. Two careful owners, low mileage, three months MOT and in reasonable condition. The salesman soon realised that I was in the trade and it didn't take much for him to knock seven hundred and fifty pounds off the price in return for not giving a warranty. My bank is used to me buying cars on the spur of the moment and the money is transferred within half an hour. Although it's not my normal sort of business, I'll be able to sell the car when I've finished with it and maybe make a couple of hundred pounds. I'm covered for insurance by my trader's policy, but it's not taxed so I'll have to take the risk. It's even got half a tank of petrol.

I need one more thing and drive back to the town centre. I'm pretty sure that a town like Ludlow has one photographic shop and that it's unlikely to have embraced the digital age. I'm spot on and find a narrow fronted shop with rows of second hand film cameras in the window, supplemented with a few dusty picture frames.

The elderly man gets irritated when I can't be precise in telling him what I want to use the binoculars for. No, they're not for bird watching or horse racing; they're for spying on a suspected Russian mafia collaborator who's taken a beautiful young woman hostage. Now just sell me a pair of bloody binoculars! In the end, he's quite pleased when I buy the most expensive pair in the shop. I pay for them on my company credit card and assume that my accountant will be his usual creative self in describing them as a legitimate business expense.

Afternoon....

I'd hardly looked at the daily route maps when I was riding. You don't need them for navigation because the route signing is so good and after the first couple of days, I lost any real interest in wanting to know where I was. But now they will be extremely useful.

Today's second stage is a long, tough ride of around forty five miles with quite a lot of hills and a final section over the old Severn Bridge. I calculate that it could take Gillian and Lawrence between four and four and a half hours, which means they will be at the second pit stop at around two thirty. I'm leaving Ludlow just before one o'clock, so should be near the second stop at roughly the same time as them. The easiest thing is to follow the blue route signs. Nobody knows the car and as long as I don't stop, there shouldn't be any problems.

I'm driving near the outskirts of Chepstow and I'm pretty certain that I've just passed Bob. He wasn't riding, he was sitting by the side of the road with his helmet off and his bike upside down on the grass verge. A hundred yards further on I pull off the road and look back at him through the binoculars. It can't be a puncture as he's not making any attempt to repair anything. I then see that his chain has broken. Tough luck. He'll have to wait for the bike mechanics' van but unfortunately, it could be a long wait. They've been totally overwhelmed by the number of breakdowns and some people have had to wait two or three hours. Others have had to be picked up by the broom wagon.

I can't decide if going back to help Bob would ruin my plan. I'm sure it might if I actually had a one. I've got as far as planning to meet up with Gillian and Lawrence somewhere near the second pit stop, for no better reason than it would be good to see them. After that, I've got to decide if I'm going to try and talk to Sinead. I've no idea where she is on the ride today and she may even have finished by now. Whatever happens, I can't be seen by Seb Johnston or any of the security guards. If I am, I have a feeling that my next ejection will be a lot more forceful. I conclude that Bob can't harm a plan that doesn't exist.

I turn the car around and park it about twenty yards from where Bob is sitting. He's looking forward and doesn't see me walk up.

"Hello Bob. What's the problem?"

If he's surprised to see me, he doesn't show it. His face looks dejected, pale and tired.

"I assumed you'd gone home," he says.

"No, I thought I'd catch the end of the ride. Anyway what's the problem - a broken chain?"

"Yes, but that's not all. It broke because the gears hit the rear wheel and buggered up a spoke. I've called event control, but they can't tell me when they can get somebody to me. Looks like it might be the broom wagon."

He pauses. "Which is a real shit. I never wanted to do this bloody ride in the first place, but having got so far, I'll be really pissed off if I haven't ridden it all."

For the first time, Bob is talking in sentences that I can understand. It's as if he's lost his shell of overacted confidence and is behaving normally.

"Well let's see if I can do anything about the bike," I say .

Spending so much time with cars means that I'm not too bad with mechanical things and by using the jack handle from the car, I'm able to lever the rear gears away from the wheel so they're no longer touching. I then start repairing the chain.

"I think I owe you a bit of an apology," Bob says. "Gillian laid into me in no uncertain terms yesterday morning. What you said at breakfast was obviously right. I didn't really mean to crowd her or anything. I actually wanted to ride with her because she rides at my speed and maybe I thought that it would look better if it seemed that I was going slowly to help her."

As an afterthought he adds. "I suppose I'm a bit clumsy when it comes to women."

"You said you didn't want to do the ride, but you're one of the proper cyclists," I say.

"I'm a Sunday morning cyclist and a pretty slow one at that, but I enjoy going out with a few of the lads from the club. Twenty or thirty miles, a cup of coffee halfway round and a couple of beers when we finish," Bob replies.

"So why do the ride then?"

" I may be a partner at Haskins, but I have bosses and one of them thought it would be a good idea if I supported the corporate cause. I suppose it was my fault in a way; I might have given them the impression that I was some kind of super cyclist."

"I can't believe that for a minute," I say mockingly.

Bob gives a rueful grin.

"Humility has never been my strongest trait."

The chain is back on the bike and I spin the pedals. The wheel moves freely and the gears just about work.

"With a bit of luck," I say, "you should get to the finish today. You won't get all the gears, but I don't want to start messing about with them. I've taken the broken spoke out. The wheel should hold up - just avoid the potholes."

Bob puts his helmet and gloves on and gets ready to go. I think about offering him a lift for a few miles, but know he won't accept.

"Thanks a lot," he says. "I really appreciate it."

"No problem," I reply. "Can you do me a favour? When you talk with the organisers about me, it would be a lot easier if you don't mention that you've seen me. I'd like to follow the ride to the end and they might make it difficult for me if they know."

Bob looks at me. "Something tells me that there's something more to this, something you're not saying. But if it makes life easier, I won't speak to them. They're unlikely to reinstate you now and you've lost a day in any case."

"Thanks, that would be good," I reply.

Bob gets on his bike. "No problem. My stomach's feeling pretty rough, so I think I'll go straight to bed as soon as I get back. Thanks again."

He rides off.

First Lawrence and now Bob - just how wrong can I be about people?

I've lost half an hour stopping for Bob and am driving over the old Severn Bridge when my phone rings. I can't afford to miss the call and there's nowhere to pull over on the bridge, so I have a quick look around for any police cars and wedge the phone under my chin.

I expect it to be Gillian, but it's Lawrence. They've just arrived at the second pit stop which is only a couple of miles from the bridge. We agree that they'll pick up some food and drink and ride a mile or so on from the stop and wait by the side of the road for me. It won't look unusual, a lot of riders stop to meet friends and relatives by the roadside.

I drive past the stop and less than a mile further on there's a village and I see Gillian and Lawrence waiting at the entrance to a pub car park.

As soon as I get out of the car Gillian rushes over to me and hugs me. She then turns away and projectile vomits over the car park. She crouches down and Lawrence hands her a water bottle.

"She's being doing that for the last twenty miles," he says. "I'm surprised there's anything left. It seems that there's a particularly virulent stomach bug going around the camp."

Gillian gets up. She's deathly white. "Sorry about that. I'll see if I can use the ladies in the pub to freshen up."

Lawrence looks at his watch. "We really want to know what happened to you, but I'm worried about the time and Gillian. We've still got to get through the centre of Bristol in the rush hour and the last few miles before the base camp is on the edge of the Cheddar Gorge and is a bit of a steep old climb. It wouldn't be easy for her at the best of times, but the way she is, I'm really not sure she can do it."

We agree that they should get going immediately and that I'll stop at a chemist to buy something to help with the sickness.

"Oh by the way," Lawrence says, "Sinead was asking if I knew where you were."

"When?"

"This morning at the first stop. I said that you'd caught the bug and couldn't ride. She seemed a bit worried about you. She hasn't got anything to do with you being thrown out, has she?"

I want to confide in Lawrence. He's a guy I can trust, but now isn't the time or place.

"Maybe indirectly. I'll explain later," I reply.

Gillian comes back out, her face dripping with water that she's sprinkled over it. She wants to talk, but Lawrence and I usher her onto her bike.

They set off and I pass them half a mile later. I sound the horn as I pass and Gillian smiles and waves. I look at her in the rear view mirror and there's a steely look of grim determination on her face. I hope her husband's boss is looking out for her.

I lay it on thick with the pharmacist. Gillian becomes my wife who is suffering from something far worse than dysentery. He stops me mid-flow and asks if she's doing the bike ride, because I'm the third person in the last hour who's come in and described the same symptoms. I leave with a bottle of thick pink gooey liquid, some anti-dehydration tablets and a recommendation that Gillian takes the gooey liquid as soon as possible. I also buy a two litre bottle of water and dissolve the tablets in the water. After a review of the route map and some simple calculations, I work out roughly where Gillian and Lawrence should be and head off to find them.

They are further back than I calculate. When I do find them, they are stopped and Gillian is vomiting over a gate into a field. Lawrence and I try to persuade her to get in the car, but she's adamant that she's going to carry on. We make her take a large swig of the gooey liquid and fill her water bottles up with the anti-dehydration solution. As I leave them again, Gillian struggles with the smile.

The quarter pounder with cheese, large fries and large Coke is going down well after six days of enforced healthy and sensible eating. I feel thinner after burning off around six thousand calories each day I rode and feel no guilt. I've driven across Bristol and out over the Clifton Suspension Bridge and can understand Lawrence's concerns for Gillian. The traffic is horrendous and although I'm now outside Bristol, I can still see lines of cars crawling along and cyclists doing their best to move past them on the inside and outside. I'm sure some of those drivers are muttering and cursing at them, but there's no way they can afford to move at the same snail-like pace as the cars.

My phone rings and Mike's name appears on the screen. I should have rung him.

"Hello Mike. How are you?"

"Fine. I didn't know whether you'd be finished by now, but you obviously have. Where are you? In the food tent having a cup of tea?"

What the hell do I say?

"Not exactly," I reply.

"So how's it all going? Only two more days to go. You must be feeling good. I'm so jealous."

"Well there's a lot to tell you Mike."

"Well don't worry now. I'll see you tomorrow."

I'd forgotten that Mike had said he was going to meet up with us.

Mike continues. "I'm going to set out early and hope to see Gillian and you at the first pit stop. I've booked a B&B in Launceston for tomorrow night so that I can follow you both all the way down to Land's End."

He sounds so excited and I can't bring myself to tell him that at the moment only one of us has a chance of finishing and that chance is looking pretty thin at the moment. I decide to wait until the morning before saying anything more.

"Mike that's great, but please ring me before you set out tomorrow morning."

I'm thinking fast. "There's talk of altering the first stage because of road works and the pit stop may move, so you must ring me. Okay?" I say.

"But what time shall I ring?"

"When you get up is probably best," I reply.

Evening....

I look at my watch - it's half past seven and there's still no sign of Gillian and Lawrence. I try to ring Lawrence again, but it keeps going to voicemail and I suspect he's turned his phone off to save the battery. I'm standing behind a hedge in a field. There's a gap in the hedge which gives me a good view through the binoculars of where the riders cross the bouncy castle finish line. I've parked the car about a quarter of a mile down the road. The route planners were obviously having a bad day when they decided on the site for the base camp, either that, or they have a very twisted sense of humour. For the last two or three miles my people carrier struggled to cope in second gear. The climb is between high walls of grey rock that do a good impression of the Cheddar Gorge and I can't see any way that Gillian will be able to do it.

It's ten past eight before I finally spot them. I re-focus the binoculars to make sure, but it is them. By moving a bit I can just see beyond the finish line and watch as Gillian gets off her bike and almost collapses into the arms of Lawrence. She doesn't move for a bit and I know that there are tears involved; lots of tears - and some of them are mine.

Back in the car, I ring Lawrence and this time he answers. He tells me that Gillian is exhausted, but all right. The pink gooey stuff stabilised things and although she had to stop quite a lot, she rode the whole way. Lawrence and I need to talk and I suggest that I walk towards the camp and we can meet halfway. This guy never ceases to amaze me! He says he fancies a run and will run to where I'm parked. I ask him if he could bring a water bottle with him.

Fifteen minutes later Lawrence is knocking on the passenger window and thirty five minutes later I've told him about Sinead, Seymour and my expulsion from the ride. His reaction is surprisingly pragmatic for a lawyer.

"You need to speak to Sinead and find out what the fuck is going on," he says.

My thoughts exactly.

"The only place I can do that is in her tent at night and it would help if I knew her tent number. There's a way you should be able to find that out for me."

"How?" Lawrence asks.

"If you say that you need to return something to rider number 345, something like tyre levers, they'll tell you her tent number."

"That seems simple enough," Lawrence replies.

We agree that he'll ring me when he's found out.

Lawrence pauses as he gets out of the car.

"So what happens next?" He asks.

"Lawrence, I have no real idea."

He nods as if I've given him a totally conclusive answer.

I do have an idea though, a plan almost. Sinead is getting out of this ride tonight.

Twenty minutes later Lawrence rings.

"I hate to add to your paranoia or start conspiracy theories, but everything was okay until the girl on the desk looked up Sinead's rider number. After that she clammed up and said they were unable to give out that rider's tent number. She then asked for my name and I said that it didn't matter. As I walked away she picked up her phone."

Night....

I'm not quite sure why they've employed so many security guards as the only thing they seem to guard is the bike compound. As soon as it gets dark they all congregate under the arc lights to smoke and chat, leaving the rest of the base camp open to looters and rapists.

There's one way not to look suspicious in the base camp at night. Everyone walks slowly, usually with a limp and carries a wash bag and water bottle. I can do the limp, I have my own wash bag and Lawrence has supplied the water bottle. As I walk towards the tent compound I have my hood up and nod and grunt as I pass people walking with a limp and carrying a wash bag and water bottle. I can see the flag of the green tent compound.

Although I don't know Sinead's tent number, I guess that it's probably going to be between one and ten. So I find number one and work my way along the row. I don't have to go too far. Outside number three is a pair of lady's cycling shoes and hanging on the tent guy ropes, a pair of shorts with a scorpion on the bum.

I should have realised that it would be relatively easy to find her tent and wonder if Sinead left the shoes and shorts out on purpose. I now regret having put Lawrence in a position where he could have the finger of suspicion pointed in his direction.

It's pretty well impossible to knock on a tent, so I try and scrape my fingers up and down the fabric in order to make some kind of noise. I try my best to whisper loudly, if there is such a noise.

"Sinead, it's Mark." No response.

More scraping.

"Sinead, it's Mark." I hear the tent zips move.

I crawl head first into the tent and can't see a thing. A torch is being shone in my face. The next thing I know, I have a sobbing woman wrapped around me. I assume it's Sinead.

The warmth, the smell. Yes, it's her.

The torch has fallen on a pile of clothes and casts a soft light around the tent.

"Thank God you came back. Richard told me that you'd been frightened off," she whispers in my ear.

As part of my plan, I've practiced this bit.

"No, well they........"

She puts her head back against mine and whispers again. "Don't talk. You can hear everything anybody says in these tents."

She's right; at night I heard every single phone call people made in their tents within a thirty yard radius. The tents seem to act like one big amplifier. So much for Plan A which was to have a talk with Sinead and find out what the hell is going on. Unfortunately, there is no Plan B.

Sinead's distracted by something and looks around. There's an arc of light flitting across the tent fabric. Someone is walking around outside with a powerful torch.

Suddenly there's a voice, a voice I recognise - No-Neck Steve. He's trying to talk quietly but fails.

"Miss O'Connor, is everyfing all right?"

Sinead grabs the torch and turns it off. "Yes fine, but why are you checking up on me?"

"Sorry, but some bloke was trying to get your tent number earlier. 'Ave you lent anyfing to anyone?"

I try and mouth the answer to her, but she can't see.

"No," she replies.

"Probly nuthin," he says. "Sorry to disturb you, saw you 'ad a light on and guessed you were still awake. Good night."

Sinead doesn't answer and we huddle together in silence. After a while she slowly unzips the tent and looks out. She turns the torch back on and mouth's *'He's gone'*.

I mouth back, 'We've got to talk'.

'I'm going to toilet'.

Christ, she does pick her moments!

She holds her hand up and faces her palm towards me. *'Five minutes - follow me'.*

Sinead has a Plan B.

I leave it four and a half minutes before crawling through the tent flap with my wash bag and water bottle. I pull the hood of my jacket over my head and look around. It's a clear night so I can see pretty well. Nobody's around in the tent compound, but I can see a few figures in the main complex. At the opposite end of the field are two individual portable toilets.

Both locks are showing green and it's second time lucky. Sinead is sitting on the lid of the toilet. They keep them reasonably clean, but I can't help but feel overpowered by the combined smell of chemicals and human waste. I've had better first dates.

We really need to talk, so we kiss - real kissing. I wonder how many people have had sex in a portable toilet? It's a nice, but passing thought. It's time to revert back to Plan A.

"Right," I say, "we obviously haven't got much time. I've got a car, so you need to pack your stuff and we can get out. We might be able to find somewhere to stay, if not, we'll have to sleep in the car."

Sinead is still hugging me as if she doesn't want to let go.

"I can't," she says.

"What the hell do you mean?"

"I mean I can't," she repeats.

"Look Sinead, if you don't come now, I'm out of here. I've stuck my neck out for you. My ride's been fucked up, I've been threatened and all because of you. You've told me sod all and unless you do, that's it. I'm going back to the real world...."

Sinead puts two fingers on my lips. There are tears in her eyes.

"Okay, you want the truth, you can have it and then you can go."

She draws a deep breath. "Richard Seymour is doing a business deal with the Trans-Global team and I'm helping him."

"So this is about selling bikes," I say, "and you're helping test them?"

"No, that's a smokescreen, a story he's put about to divert attention."

"Divert attention from what?" I ask

"Drugs."

Shit!

"You are joking?"

I know that it's a rhetorical question.

By some devilish curse of timing, someone goes into the toilet next to us and we are immediately subjected to a bombardment of unbelievably loud bodily function noises. We look at one another and start giggling. She's just told me that she involved in some kind of drugs racket and I'm giggling. We can't look at one another and hug. Both of us shaking with laughter and trying desperately to stifle any noise.

As quickly as it began, the aural assault ends and we stop laughing as if we're controlled by some kind of switch.

"So what sort of drugs?" I ask. "Heroin, cocaine - that sort?"

"Christ no. P.E.D.s"

"What?"

"P.E.D.s. - Performance Enhancing Drugs. Drugs for the Trans-Global bike team to use. Richard's brokering a big deal with the Russians to supply some new wonder drug that can't be detected by the drug testing agencies."

I'm not sure if this is good news or not.

"So where do you fit in? Why are you involved?"

"They're using the ride to field test the drug and I'm taking the blood and urine samples every morning and evening. The Russians are taking their own samples, but the suppliers insisted that Richard arrange for independent samples to be taken by somebody who knows what they're doing and can do it without the risk of contamination. They're worried that Trans-Global will alter the results to show that the drug isn't as good as the suppliers say and knock the price down.

I've so many questions. "But why you?" I ask.

"Because I'm a nurse and a cyclist."

This only answers a fraction of what I want to know, but I realise we can't stay in this stinking toilet for much longer.

"So you're not coming with me?"

"I can't. The ride is giving them only nine days of results; the big tour events are longer and anything less than nine days will be practically worthless. If I go now there'll be some very angry men. There's an awful lot of money riding on this. I tried to get out as soon as I realised what was going on, but it was made very clear that if I did, I was risking everything - my job, my family and the ability to ride a bike."

The tears which were in her eyes are now running down her cheeks.

"Please don't leave," she says. "Just wait until the ride is over and I'll tell you everything. You've got to believe me - I didn't get into this intentionally. Richard Seymour's tricked me and used me."

She's well and truly called my bluff. The last thing I'm going to do now is get in my people carrier and drive back into my old world. Sinead is my new world.

"No, I won't leave. But can we meet up on the ride tomorrow somewhere?" I ask.

"It's difficult," she replies. "He's put a tracker on my bike so he can keep an eye on me. He knows when I stop and if I stop for too long, he'll come and find out why. But on the first stage tomorrow, he'll be going to Bristol to send the samples off. He'll see I've stopped, but won't be able to check why. I'll tell him that I had a puncture."

I describe the car to her and we agree that around twenty miles into the first stage, I'll drive past and stop somewhere ahead. All we'll have is the time it takes to fix a puncture, which is around fifteen minutes, but at least it's something.

We kiss goodbye and she leaves. I wait another five minutes before limping back across the field carrying my wash bag and water bottle.

Day Eight

Morning...

I've no idea what the time is when I stumble out of the car to have a pee. The base camp must be a quarter of a mile away, but I can hear the wake up music. It's a familiar tune - a Coldplay song and the chorus is repeating over and over again. I know the words - *Nobody said it was easy. No one ever said it would be this hard. Oh, take me back to the start.* The person choosing the wake up music hasn't lost their sense of humour, but I wonder if Gillian is laughing this morning.

There's nothing like a good night's sleep and that was nothing like a good night's sleep. Even by fully reclining the front passenger seat, the inside of the people carrier didn't transform itself into the equivalent of a first class plane cabin. Not that I've ever travelled first class. *She* occasionally did when she travelled for work and if not first class, it was always business class. Something she continually reminded me of every time we flew in economy together.

I haven't thought about *her* for days. Is this is a turning point? A day didn't go by without me blaming her for whatever had gone wrong in my life, no matter how small and trivial. It's amazing how I could find a way to make *her* responsible for something insignificant like running out of milk or forgetting to take the rubbish out.

I haven't been thinking of *her* because I've been thinking of Sinead. Sinead is my new *she* and *her* and I'm convinced that *she's* going to be the reason for everything going right in my life.

I try to get some more sleep before the start of the ride at seven o'clock and am just dozing off when my phone rings. Who the hell is ringing me at this time in the morning?

"Good morning Mark," Mike says. His brightness at this hour in the morning is unnatural and irritating. "You're obviously up then, have you packed yet or are you on the way to breakfast?"

I realise that I don't know if Gillian is going to be riding today, but I can't mess Mike about anymore.

"Mike, Gillian had a very bad stomach bug yesterday and I'm not sure if she'll be able to ride today and I probably should have told you before, but I'm no longer riding."

I'm getting better at summarising the story and it only takes a few minutes to tell Mike what's happened. I include Richard Seymour, but just say that he got upset because he thought I was coming on to his wife. This gets Mike's seal of approval and obviously makes the whole story plausible.

"So Mike," I say, " it's up to you if you want to drive down."

"Well, I've arranged to pick up my bike from the base camp in Launceston tonight, so I've got to do that, but maybe I'll come down later this afternoon. I've paid for the room in the B&B, so I might as well use it. I'll go back to bed now."

He sounds a bit grumpy, but I'm sure he's just disappointed. I feel guilty. I should have said something last night. At least he could have had a lie in.

At seven o'clock I'm back at my gap in the hedge looking through the binoculars at the start line. Dead on time the air horn blows and riders are released in groups of about twenty, each one receiving a briefing about the route and a reminder not to upset the natives by peeing in their front gardens. It's going to be another tough day of one hundred and seven miles. You might be fooled into thinking that after Scotland and the Lake District, the worst hills were behind you and that the West Country would be the equivalent of a ride in the park. However, the road builders in the north were sensible and generally built their roads with constant gradients and routed them around the mountains and hills. In Devon and Cornwall they obviously decided that it would be much more fun to go straight up one side of a hill and down the other, then when they got to the bottom and were faced with another hill, they did exactly the same thing again, and then again and then again.

The fourth group are released and I see Lawrence and Gillian and then Bob! He's obviously riding with them as once they're on the road they bunch up together. It's really great to see that Gillian's riding, but I'm struggling with the concept of Bob riding with her.

Half an hour later, Sinead rides out with a number of serious looking club riders and I follow her with the binoculars. The scorpion can't see me and merely gyrates rhythmically with each movement of her bum. Once she's gone I run back to the car. There's a way I can avoid the ride route for about fifteen miles and then rejoin it. When I do, I'll stop and wait for her to go past, but I need to get a move on, fifteen miles at the speed they cycle will take less than forty five minutes.

Every bloody rider looks the same. I very nearly miss them, but remember that the lead guy is wearing a very loud orange jersey. It seems the better you get at cycling, the more outlandish the clothes you wear. I have to push the people carrier to keep up with them and the road is twisting and narrow, which makes it difficult to overtake the line of cyclists. Finally, there's a clear section of road and I press the accelerator to the floor to overtake. My God, I didn't know they still made cars that are so underpowered. A car comes from the other direction and I'm forced to tuck in behind Sinead. As I hover behind her back wheel, she lifts her right hand slightly to acknowledge me. I finally get past and start looking for somewhere to stop.

A mile further on the road is straighter and I stop by a farm entrance. The verge has been used for parking and I can pull off the road yet still be seen. I sit in the car and watch in the rear view mirror as the orange jersey come into view and then passes. Sinead passes and brakes.

I hear her shout, "Puncture - go on."

Two riders behind her go past, wave an acknowledgement and follow the riders ahead. Sinead pushes her bike around to the side of the car so that it's hidden from the road and gets into the passenger seat.

She's smiling and we kiss.

"You look happier," I say.

"Well there's only one day left after this. I thought it would never end, but it will soon *and* I've got you."

Sinead is beautiful when she's angry and upset, which are really the only ways I've seen her, but when she's happy and smiling she's..., well just amazing.

"You haven't changed your mind then? I ask. "We can just drive away now and you can put all this behind you."

Her angry face returns. "How many times do I have to tell you? I can't, so please just drop it."

We haven't got very long and I don't want to spoil what time we have got by arguing. I change the subject.

"Okay, okay, not another word. So tell me about your family," I say.

Her face calms.

"Well it's not very big; me, my son Danny and my barmy gambling mother."

"How old's your son?"

"He's ten. He hates cycling, but loves cars and motor racing."

She smiles. "He's pretty impressed with you. Driven at Le Mans twice, Porsche Cup winner, Touring Cars and Historic Car Racing."

"How the hell does he know all that?"

"Because I ring him every night and I told him that I'd met a racing driver, so he looked you up on the Internet," she replies.

"I'm flattered, he's probably the only person who ever has. Does your mother live with you?"

"Yes, I'm afraid so. She has a slight problem with dementia and is totally addicted to Internet poker or any kind of gambling come to that."

I laugh, but Sinead doesn't laugh with me. "If it wasn't for her I wouldn't be doing this bloody ride. We must be the only household in the country where a ten year old has set up a parental lock on the computer to stop their grandmother from gambling away the family money."

Sinead looks at her watch. "I must go."

"So can we meet again this afternoon or tonight?"

"No way, one puncture is okay, but any more stops and he'll become suspicious. Please stay away until this is all over. It's not that long."

"And then you'll tell me everything?"

She kisses me. "Everything. I promise."

I'd agreed with Lawrence that he'd ring me when they reached the first stop and we'd then meet up somewhere close by. I drive past the stop, park in a car park next to a petrol station and wait for his call.

My phone rings. "Hello Lawrence. Where are you?"

"Mark is that you? It's Peter Jeffries."

Shit! I hadn't looked at the screen and had forgotten about Sir Peter Jeffries.

"Sorry Peter, I was expecting a call from someone else."

"Clearly, now what's all this fuss with Haskins about? Stella tells me you've upset one their partners."

I need to divert Peter's attention away from the argument with Bob. It wouldn't be fair if he complained to Haskins about him. I tell him that the real problem was a man called Richard Seymour who'd overreacted to a friendship I'd struck up with his wife who I'd met whilst riding. I say that Seymour had accused me of harassing her and the organisers had taken his word against mine, that there was a big argument and I was excluded from the ride.

"Well that certainly doesn't sound like you Mark," Sir Peter says.

"No, that's the point, but I'm sorry Peter; I shouldn't have used your name."

"Don't worry about that my boy. It's a pity I wasn't around to help out."

I hear the tone that somebody else is ringing me and realise it's probably Lawrence. I need to politely get rid of Sir Peter.

"Well, it's water under the bridge now. It would be nice to get a refund of some kind, but no doubt the small print stops that happening," I say.

"I need to talk to one of Haskin's senior partners this morning so I will mention it to him. After all they did try to contact to me. I wouldn't think he'll know anything about it, but it might help if you want to take it further. What was the name of the Haskin's partner you had the other argument with?"

"Sorry Peter," I reply, "I don't know, but that was more of a misunderstanding. It just didn't help at the time."

"Okay, so where are you now?" he asks.

I tell him that I'm following the ride and keeping in touch with people I've met. I hear another incoming call notification and I try to end the conversation, but Sir Peter wants to talk about motor racing.

It's another five minutes before I ring back Lawrence. They've left the pit stop and will reach me in a few minutes.

Gillian gets off her bike slowly and we hug. I notice that Bob is holding back.

"So how are you?" I ask.

"Better than yesterday. The stuff you got worked and don't ask me how, but I managed to finish. I went straight to my tent and slept right through. The problem is I can't face food and haven't eaten anything."

"Do you want me to get you some more medicine?" I ask.

"That's very sweet of you, but the doctor at the camp gave me some sachets of powder to put in my water bottles. I've just got to keep drinking. You should have seen the queue; the doctor was handing them out like lollipops to kids."

Gesturing towards Bob I say, "Why the hell is Bob riding with you?"

"I felt sorry for him. He's got the bug, although not as bad as me and you know that he had trouble with his bike. Since we had our little chat he's been really nice - friendly, but not clinging or touchy feely."

"You're a big softy," I reply.

Gillian smiles. "Me? What about you Sir Galahad? Rescuing the beautiful young damsel."

"So Lawrence told you?" I say glancing across at Bob.

"Yes, but Bob doesn't know anything. Anyway, I don't think I've seen this girl and I need to know what the competition is like. I thought you were devoted to me, I'm really upset."

"Sorry, I can cope with husbands," I glance upwards, "but not their bosses."

We hug again and then I go over to Bob.

"How's the bike and how are you?" I ask.

"The bike's in better shape than me. The mechanics replaced the spoke, put a new hanger on the gears and adjusted them, but I feel rubbish."

I touch him on the arm as I walk away. "Stick in there - you'll make it."

I watch as the three of them ride off. They are going to finish the ride, but I'm not and I feel dejected. If it was adrenalin that was keeping me going, it's just drained away. I'm hungry, tired, haven't washed for twenty four hours and I've failed. After all the months of preparation and training, whichever way you look at it, I've failed. I've already made up the excuse of a bad knee to satisfy my friends and family, but I know the truth. This was going to be my one success after months and months of failure and now it's just something else to add to the list.

There's Sinead, but I've been here before. Blindly in love, only for it to fall to pieces when reality takes hold. It took about four years before the decay started before, but this time there's so much more to learn. So much I don't know about Sinead. This time it could all disintegrate in a couple of days. Perhaps that's what love is - nothing more than an ephemeral experience. Maybe I shouldn't expect that it can be something more.

What do I do now? It's mid morning and there's a day and a half before the finish. I can't see Sinead again and I can't expect Gillian, Lawrence and Bob to keep making unscheduled stops. They have their own challenge and for the next day and a half I'm not going to be part of their world.

Mike will be company when he arrives, but he'll have his rider's pass and be able to get into the pit stops and base camp, whereas all I can do is look on from a distance through a pair of binoculars.

I ring Mike to get the phone number of his B&B and manage to book a room for tonight. I head back to a Little Chef I passed earlier. An Olympic Breakfast might lift my spirits, but I'll have to pay for it this time.

Just as the breakfast is put in front of me my phone rings. It's Sir Peter and I'm tempted to reject the call. He'll want to talk about cars and racing and I'll struggle to concentrate, but this the real world; a world I've got to go back to and I can't afford to ignore an important client.

"Mark, I've just had a very interesting chat with Leonard Avery of Haskin. It appears that they're in a bit of a flap over their Long Britain Ride. This must remain totally confidential, but the Anti-Doping Agency, the people who deal with sports drugs, have been in touch with them and said that they've received a tip-off that the ride is being used by a Russian cycling team to test drugs."

Shit! Shit! Shit!

Sir Richard continues. "Even more interesting is that the gentlemen who was instrumental in getting you thrown out, Richard Seymour, is thought to be somehow involved."

My head is spinning, my stomach is churning and my voice sounds weak.

"So what are they going to do about it?"

"Well that's why they're in a bit of a flap. Nobody at Haskin really knows too much detail about the ride because they've left the organisation to a fund-raising company called CCF. Anybody in Haskin who might know something are taking part in the ride. They are desperate to keep it quiet. You can imagine how it would affect their image if this got out."

So why is Sir Peter telling me and why have they told him?

"But they've told you," I say.

"Well I could say it's because I'm a non-excec, but that's not the reason. It's because of you."

"Because of me?" I say. "What's it got to do with me?" I hope I don't sound too defensive.

"At first Leonard didn't say anything and only mentioned it after I told him what had happened to you. Leonard believes that you could be of assistance to them."

"Assistance - how?" I ask.

"The Anti-Doping Agency want to catch the Russians red handed, but Leonard's embarrassed that Haskin know very little about the detail of the event. The Agency suspect that this CCF company might be involved in some way, so have told Haskin not to contact them or anybody who's doing the ride. If they are going to catch them, they need to make sure it stays secret.

This is becoming a very, very bad dream.

"I still don't see where I figure in all this," I say, hoping that I don't sound too hysterical.

"Haskin want you to act as their ears and eyes so they can answer whatever questions the Agency throw at them. They want to be seen to be giving them full cooperation.

I start to stutter, "I'm not too sure....."

Sir Peter butts in. "I've vouched for your good character and all that and said that it would be best if all communications comes through me. It keeps you at arm's length."

"But Peter, why do you want to be involved?" I ask.

"Dear boy, I don't want to miss out on all the excitement. I've been rattling on for ages at our non-excec meetings about how out of touch Haskin's senior management are, but nobody's listens. I'm going to make a bit of hay and have a bit of fun over this."

"*If* I agree to this, how will it all work?" I ask.

"I'm not too sure about the exact detail. Haskin have said that they'll cooperate with the Agency, but don't want to spoil the public relations circus they've organised for the finish at Land's End. The Agency are putting their plans together and will require information from Haskin. If Haskin don't know the answers, they'll pass it on to me and I'll contact you."

I'm trying to think and don't reply, but Sir Peter presses. "Mark, I've got to get back to Leonard and tell him whether you'll help. You never know, there might be a sponsorship deal from Haskin in all this. They're in a big hole and will be very grateful to anybody who helps pull them out."

Cunning sod; he never misses an angle. "Okay, I'll help, provided I can back out at any time if I'm not happy."

"Wonderful dear boy. I'll be back in touch."

I look at my cold Olympic Breakfast and I'm not hungry anymore. In fact I feel sick.

In any other car I'd be worried about driving on the outside lane of the motorway with the accelerator pedal pushed into the carpet, but the people carrier can only go over the speed limit by a tiny bit and hopefully not enough to worry any cruising police car or laser hairdryer operator. Anyway, points on my license are the last thing I'm worried about. My instinct tells me that I've got to speak to Sinead, or at least open up some line of communication. I haven't got enough time to get to the second pit stop and have worked out a route along the M5 and A30 that should get me to the base camp at Launceston before her. I haven't worked out what I'm going to do when I get there, but I bought some paper and envelopes at the Little Chef and have written her a note.

'Sinead ring me on 07886 821680. It's URGENT AND SERIOUS. You've got to believe me - we cannot wait until the finish'.

I'm assuming she must have a phone because told me about ringing her son.

Afternoon...

I make good progress and find the base camp which is in the middle of the town. It's not like the previous camps and is based at a school. The tents are pitched on the school field, but it looks like the food and everything else is in the school buildings. I'm early and the mat that the riders ride over to trigger the timing system is being laid out and connected to the laptop by my favourite timing girl. The advantage of the camp being in the middle of the town is that there are a lot of people milling around so I feel inconspicuous. I park the car a couple of streets away and walk back to the camp entrance.

The girl is now sitting at the table behind the laptop.

"Hello, remember me?" I say.

It takes her a couple of seconds to recognise me out of cycling clothes.

"Yes, of course. What's happened, why aren't you riding?"

"Buggered my knee. You couldn't do me a favour in the course of true love."

She smiles. "Rider 345, O'Connor?"

"That's the one. Can you give her this? I hand her the envelope. My phone battery is dead and I need to find a physio. I need to let her know."

"Of course, but I can just tell her."

I think quickly. "Well there's something else that I want to tell her in the envelope."

"You old romantic. Yes of course I can do that," she says.

I thank her and remember to limp as I walk away.

The lady at the B&B was surprised when I arrived early, but my room was ready and she said I could use it straight away.

It's a much nicer room than the one in Ludlow. Floral wallpaper with matching bed linen and lampshades, a pink en-suite and a kettle with everything to make a cup of tea. The sun is shining through the window which overlooks a neat, well tended garden. This is a little bit of heaven and a bit of me wishes that I could lock the door and stay here forever.

Then the bloody phone rings. It's a number that isn't recognised.

"Mark Anthony," I answer.

"It's me. What the hell is this all about?"

It's a long time since I've had a '*me*'. Sinead is now *her, she* and *me.*

"I'm afraid I can't tell you at the moment. I can tell you the problem, but not the solution. You do have to totally trust me now. We need to meet, but I need to work out how. Can you ring me at seven?"

"No, I'll be with him."

"When can you ring?"

"It's difficult."

Bloody hell, there's just one person making this difficult.

"Listen Sinead, Mr Richard Seymour and his shady little deal are about to be blown out of the water and if you don't ring me later, you'll go with him and I won't be around to pick up the pieces. So let's do this again. What time can you ring?"

"After eight."

"I'll speak to you then."

It never ceases to amaze me how small plastic kettles can generate so much noise when they're boiling such tiny amounts of water. It's so loud it almost drowns out the sound of my phone ringing. I miss Sir Peter's call and I decide that I'm going to lie down and drink my cup of tea before doing anything else. Despite everything, I finish my tea and fall asleep.

Inevitably, Sir Peter rings back.

"Mark, I've heard back from Leonard. The Anti-Doping Agency have now involved the International Cycling Federation and they are planning to carry out a surprise drug test on the Trans-Global riders. Apparently under a new biological passport system that professional teams have to sign up to, they've got the right to carry out tests even when riders aren't competing."

"When are they planning to do that?" I ask.

"Ah, that's where you come in. Haskin don't want them to do it at the end and spoil the party, but the Agency people can't get their side ready until around midday. They were thinking of the second stop at Truro. Haskins have got the details of where it is, but don't know what time the team will get there."

"There are a couple of problems with that," I reply. "Firstly, the Trans-Global riders don't stop at the intermediate stops. They get food and drink from their support vehicles and don't use the event timing. They just ride straight past. Secondly, they run to their own timetable so you can't be totally sure where they'll be at any one time."

"Right, that obviously is a problem. I'll pass that back. It's just as well you're on board. The Agency also need to know a bit more about your friend

Richard Seymour. They want to know what his connection is with the event. Is he riding?"

I need to take a very deep breath.

"No, he's not riding. He's supporting his wife who is doing the ride. That's how I met her."

"So you don't know anything more than that."

"No."

"Okay, I'll pass all that on and give you a ring back later."

I need to have a good look at the base camp so I can work out how to meet Sinead later and decide to walk from the B&B. When I get close to the camp entrance the main body of riders are arriving. They've attracted a crowd who are cheering and clapping each rider in. It's easy enough to mingle, but I can't get into the camp. There is a residential road which runs parallel to the entrance and then rises up above the school playing fields. I walk up it and look down onto the field where the tents are pitched. To get to the road from the field you have to climb up a grass bank, but that won't be a problem for Sinead. Although there's a fence, there are quite a few holes in it; no doubt it's used as a short cut by the school children. It's an ideal meeting place.

I'm just about to leave my room to meet up with Mike who's just arrived, when Sir Peter rings again. He's passed the details of our previous conversation on and been told that the Agency want to get hold of the actual drugs so they can analyse them. They are trying to get the help of the Customs who have stop and search powers if they believe drugs or pharmaceuticals have been brought into the country illegally. They want to know the registration number of Richard Seymour's Range Rover so they can search it. I can remember the number and tell him.

I stop him hanging up.

"Has anything been said about Seymour's wife?" I ask.

"No I just passed on what you told me. Why?"

"Oh I just wondered. It's just that she's a nice girl... and I can't believe that she's got herself mixed up in all this"

Sir Peter picks up on my hesitation.

"Mark, is there something you're not telling me?" Sir Peter asks.

I take a very deep breath. "There is something Peter, but it's not clear at the moment. You're going to have to trust me on this for a bit. I would be grateful if you could let me know if anything is said about Seymour's wife or if she's being implicated in any way."

"I'm not sure I'm comfortable with this," he says. "But for the moment I'll cut you a bit of slack."

"Thanks. Can I ring you later?"

"Of course dear boy, I hardly sleep."

Evening....

The pint I'm drinking tastes good. Mike and I have met up and are having an early evening drink in a pub in the town centre. I'm keeping a look-out for No-Neck Steve and his drinking pals and hope he hasn't got another night off. Mike is looking ruddy and in rude health and so much better than when I last saw him. The cut on his chin has healed well and there's only a small plaster covering it. I've ducked and dived his more probing questions and have found that Mike's train of thought is quickly diverted by getting the conversation back to Gillian's chest.

The conversation starts veering into tricky areas again so I try and move it away.

"So you're picking up your bike from the camp this evening?" I say.

"I hope so," Mike replies. "They seem a bit vague as to where it is. They think it's on the trailer behind the broom wagon. If not it's in some depot somewhere. Anyway, I've brought my old bike just in case."

"Just in case of what?"

"In case they haven't got my bike. Didn't I tell you? I'm going to ride tomorrow."

"Mike, please tell me you're joking."

He smiles. "Not all of it. I'll try the middle stage and see how I get on."

I shake my head in a mixture of disbelief and admiration.

It's nearly half past eight and I'm lying on the bed in the B&B, but there's no chance that I'll fall asleep this time. The phone rings - it's Sinead.

I describe the road that runs parallel with the school field and tell her that I'll be parked there after ten o'clock when it's dark. There are no questions or discussion.

I park at five minutes before ten and before I've put the handbrake on, Sinead opens the front passenger door and jumps in. There are no hugs or kisses. She sits facing forward looking straight ahead as I tell her about my phone calls with Sir Peter Jeffries. By the time I've finished tears are streaming down her face, but she still doesn't look at me.

"That's it then," she says. "That's me well and truly screwed. No money, no job or career, just my bloody mother's gambling debts."

"Look," I say "if we are to stand any chance of getting you out of this, you've got to be totally honest with me. Sir Peter's a powerful man who can pull strings, but I can't afford to lie to him. If I don't tell him the truth, my livelihood is on the line. Do you understand?"

She nods.

"What do you want to know? It's a long story and I'm frightened of being away from the tent for too long."

"Okay, I'll be as quick as I can, but I'm going to be direct as we haven't got time for niceties. Is that okay?"

She nods again.

"How do you know Richard Seymour?"

Sinead sniffs and rubs a tear away from her cheek.

"He sold imported surgical instruments to the hospital where I worked. He used to wine and dine the nurses and doctors in order to get them to put pressure on the hospital to buy his instruments."

"But he doesn't do that anymore?"

"No. He became the European distributor for a Malaysian company that manufactures sports nutrition products, drinks, gels, energy bars and that kind of thing. I think he made better money out of that and dropped the surgical instrument business."

"And he comes from Dorking?" I say.

She turns and looks at me. "How did you know that?"

"It doesn't matter now. So how did you end up doing the ride?"

"I hadn't seen him for some time and then he rang up one day and wanted to take me out for lunch. He told me that his company wanted to use the Haskin ride as a field trial for a new electrolyte energy drink and that he'd done a deal with Trans-Global to use their cyclists. The trial required daily blood and urine samples to be taken from the riders which were then to be sent for analysis. Richard doesn't cycle, but remembered my past and asked if I'd enter the ride with him posing as my husband. The ride doesn't allow commercial activities, so he wanted to use me as cover."

"So you said yes just like that? You were happy to ride a thousand miles just to do him a favour?"

"No, I needed the money."

"So he paid you?"

"Yes, it was a business arrangement. His company would publicise the results of the tests and use them to sell millions of bottles of the stuff. It's a very large and lucrative market. I couldn't see any harm, these drinks are not drugs and he told me that one of the reasons for the test was to publish proper evidence which proved that the drink didn't break any rules."

"So when did you find out that it wasn't sports drinks that they were testing?" I ask.

"On the first morning. It was totally obvious. When I got back from the ride I told him that I wasn't going to be involved and was leaving. That was when he made the threats to me and said he'd tip off the Royal College of Nursing and that they'd kick me out for unprofessional conduct, which would mean no job and no money. He played it hard ball."

This whole conversation sounds like an interrogation, probably because that is what it has to be. It's also got to end with a lot unanswered questions. I take hold of both her hands and for the first time she turns and faces me. Her eyes are grey, her face is streaked with dried tears and she looks petrified. If Sinead isn't telling the truth, she's a bloody good actress.

She asks the most obvious and difficult question.

"So what's going to happen?"

The truthful answer of '*I haven't got the faintest idea*' would do nothing to allay her fears.

"I'm going to speak to Sir Peter. He's in contact with Haskin and so may have found some more about what's happening tomorrow."

Her eyes are saying '*and.....?*'

I have no '*and... '* The only answer I can give is a crap one.

"We'll work something out." I say. "Keep your phone on all the time - it is fully charged isn't it?"

She nods.

"And look out for the car, if it's parked by the roadside - stop."

I kiss her cheek, but she doesn't respond. Without saying anything she gets out of the car and disappears back down the bank.

Night...

There's not much chance I'll sleep tonight. I've rung Sir Peter and told him exactly what Sinead had told me. He listened without making any comments or asking any questions, which was unnerving. He said that he would need time to think. He didn't know any more about the Anti-Doping Agency's plans and said he would ring early in the morning.

My thoughts are going round and round.

I know it's not right. It can't be, it's cheating and you don't cheat in sport. Or you shouldn't. The problem is that one man's cheating is another man's interpretation of the rules. In motor racing there's no point in the driver taking drugs, so the cheating has to be, and is different. An extra degree or two on the spoiler angle, a change in air restrictor, an additive to the fuel...the list is endless. Have I knowingly cheated in a race? Define knowingly. I've had my suspicions that the team may have made an unusual modification, but have I ever faced up to them and asked? Have I ever walked out and given up everything in a fit of righteous indignation? Athletes '*taking drugs*' is such an emotive term and automatically conjures up images of a back alleys and needles, yet in motor racing '*interpreting the rules differently*' is totally benign.

My brain won't stop - it's going to be a long night.

Day Nine

Morning....

Not being able to sleep was unsurprisingly a self-fulfilling prophesy. Instead of counting sheep, I've spent the night thinking up suitable wake up music. Not for the riders, but for me. All of which is a little perverse as I won't be asleep. At four o'clock the shortlist is, *'The Drugs Don't Work'*, *Always Look on the Bright Side of Life, Riders on the Storm* and *Addicted to Love.* If it all goes tits up today, perhaps I can get a job as the wake-up music man for next year's ride.

It's half past six and I'm back in the road which overlooks the base camp. I risk looking through the binoculars and hope that I'm not reported as being a pervert or voyeur and will be dismissed as an early morning bird spotter. I can see the tents in the green compound, but there's no sign of Sinead. The whole place is a hive of activity as riders pack their bags and leave their tents for the last time. It must be a wonderful feeling.

Sir Peter rings whilst I'm watching Gillian, Lawrence and Bob edge slowly towards the bouncy castle start line.

"Sorry to ring you so early, but I assumed you'd be up and about," he says. "I've been giving some thought as to the best way to help your young lady."

It's an encouraging start. It sounds like he's believed what I told him.

He continues. "My first idea was to talk to Haskin and the Agency and say that she's an innocent who's unwittingly become embroiled with this man Seymour. But the more I thought about it, I decided she isn't."

"Isn't what?" I ask.

"An innocent, dear boy. Whichever way you look at it, she's entered a charity event which shouldn't be used for commercial purposes, with the intention of doing just that. Plus, she's misrepresented herself as being Seymour's wife. I accept that a sports drink is more palatable than performance enhancing drugs, but some might argue that the deceit is still there."

I realise that men like Sir Peter haven't become successful by looking at the world or people through rose tinted glasses. I'm beginning to feel deflated. I was pinning my hopes on Sir Peter waving some kind of magic wand.

"So does that mean you can't do anything?" I ask.

Sir Peter pauses briefly. "You're obviously quite taken with this young lady and I'm sure she has her reasons for getting involved, so the best I can do is give you some advice."

"That would be good. Thank you."

"I'd get her out of the ride before the Agency and the Customs chaps jump all over this Trans-Global lot and Seymour. If she's around they'll start asking her questions and even if she convinces them that she was forced into helping Seymour, the fact that she's a nurse will no doubt come out. Once that happens they'll almost certain to refer it to the Royal College of Nursing and she'll no doubt face a disciplinary hearing."

"But won't it look suspicious if she's gone?" I ask.

"Maybe, but all they know is that Seymour's got a wife who's doing the ride. They may not even be interested in her. Remember performance enhancing drugs are not like Class A and B drugs and they are unlikely to be illegal in terms of the law. Having said that, I still think it's best if she's not around; out of sight, out of mind and all that."

Sir Peter has just told me something which hadn't crossed my mind before.

"So does that mean that Seymour will get away with it?"

"The Customs might be interested if he's imported pharmaceuticals or chemicals illegally, but it will probably be too costly to bring it to court. So in reality, your young lady has probably the most to lose and that's why it's best that she quietly disappears."

This is all becoming a bit crazy.

"So what will this operation actually achieve?"

"The Anti-Doping Agency and the cycling federation want to catch Trans-Global with a smoking gun. If they do, Trans-Global will be thrown out of competitive cycling. It will also show how well this biological passport system works and act as a deterrent to others. Also, if they can get hold of the drug, they can analyse it and improve their detection methods."

I can see how all that is good for the sport, but I need to focus on a more specific problem.

"So have they worked out how they are going to pull in the Trans-Global team?" I ask.

"Yes, they've got the Truro police to help as they are allowed to assist the Customs people. Just past the Truro stop there is a lorry park and the police will direct the Trans-Global riders and support cars into it. And that's where they hope you will be able to help."

"How? What do they want me to do?"

"Are you able to follow the Trans-Global team so the Agency has some idea when to expect them? The police can't sit around waiting all day and Haskin don't want them to be too conspicuous. They want it to be quick and clinical with a minimum of fuss. So if you can let them know, say fifteen minutes before Trans-Global get to the stop, they can be ready for them."

Shit! How am I going to get Sinead out of the ride and follow the team? I could of course refuse, but I don't. Sir Peter tells me that somebody will ring me from the Anti-Doping agency and that I'm to liaise with them. He says goodbye and wishes me luck.

I assimilate what Sir Peter has said and realise that there's another big problem. The only way to pull Sinead out of the ride before the second stop is to stop or divert her whilst she's riding, but as soon as that happens, Seymour will see it on his tracker. If her bike stops and doesn't start moving after a bit or goes off the route, he'll immediately get suspicious and try and find her. It won't take him long to realise that something is wrong and warn the Trans-Global team. I'm not sure what the team could do, but they may well have some kind of contingency plan. Whatever happens, I can't believe that Seymour will stick around for long.

I can't tell Sir Peter. I'm sure he wouldn't stick with his suggestion of Sinead pulling out if there was any chance that it would jeopardise the operation. His loyalty is with Haskin. Although he might be taking pleasure from their embarrassment, they pay him a lot of money for being a non-executive and he's not going to bite the hand that feeds him. He wants to ensure there is damage limitation, with him taking the credit.

All of this leads to an uncomfortable conclusion. I am the only outside person who knows about the Agency's plan. If it all goes pear shaped, fingers will be pointed at me and Sir Peter put in a very embarrassing position. I'm under no illusion that if that happened, he would make quite sure that I never drive in anything more exciting than a banger race and end up selling Fiestas to spotty youths.

I have another look at the start line to see if I can see Sinead. I can't, but notice Mike among the small crowd of people. I ring him.

"Mike, have you got your car with you?"

"Yes, it's parked down the road."

Five minutes later Mike pulls up in a Subaru Impreza Turbo with two bikes on the roof.

"That's quite a car for a seventy year old," I say. Mike is sitting in the passenger seat of the people carrier.

"Yes. I've always liked my cars and the women love the Subaru," he chuckles. "It's a lot better than this old heap; you'll never pull women in this."

I only want to pull one.

I have to tell Mike the whole story and fill in the gaps that I'd previously glossed over. When I've finished I have one question for Mike.

"So Mike, do you think you could follow the Trans-Global team when they leave and keep me updated by phone? I'll be honest it won't be easy. These guys don't hang about."

Mike smiles. "Have you forgotten what I used to do?"

I struggle, the coach journey from Inverness seems a lifetime away. "You were in the Met police."

"Yes and what did I do?" He doesn't wait for a reply. "I was a traffic cop and spent most of my time driving high performance police cars. I've done every advanced driving test there is, so I don't think I'll have any trouble keeping up with a bunch of cyclists."

It's been a long time since something has fallen so neatly into place.

"You'll have to follow them all the way to the second stop," I say, "so you won't have much chance to cycle today."

"Don't worry, this sounds like much more fun," he replies.

I need to get to the first pit stop as quickly as possible. There's no alternative to using the ride route which goes around the edge of Bodmin Moor, past Camelford and down to the stop south of Padstow. The road would be okay if it wasn't full of bloody cyclists and I wish I had Mike's Subaru so I can get past them more easily.

I've no idea if Sinead has left before me, but my main concern is finding Lawrence who has become the linchpin of my developing plan. About three miles before the stop I pass Lawrence, Gillian and Bob. Lawrence is riding alongside Gillian with Bob riding behind. I sound the horn as I drive past and they acknowledge me.

It looks like a lot of friends and family of riders have come to follow the last day and the pit stop is busy. I take a chance, park on the road and walk back to the timing desk.

"Hello, me again..."

The girl smiles, doesn't say anything and scrolls through the computer screen.

"She left about an hour ago, so she should be here in around half an hour, maybe a bit less."

The girls calls after me as I walk away.

"That physio worked a miracle."

What the hell is she talking about?..Shit, of course the physio.

"Err.. yes. Worth every penny." I reply.

I'm unable to resist the overwhelming compulsion to start limping, albeit not as badly as yesterday.

I find somewhere to park about half a mile past the stop and ring Lawrence. Twenty minutes later the three of them are with me. Gillian wants to talk, but I don't have time. I need to talk to Lawrence by himself. I practically drag him around to the back of the car.

Five minutes later I'm explaining to Gillian and Bob as best as I can, that Lawrence won't be riding with them any longer. Gillian is totally bewildered and asks more and more questions and I'm extremely grateful when Bob ushers her away. She seems quite happy to go with him which is quite a turnaround from a few days ago.

To make absolutely sure Sinead stops, I stand by the back of the car. Lawrence is sitting in the front passenger seat and his disassembled bike is stowed in the back.

After an interminable wait, I see her amongst a group of riders. Before she gets to me she stops and shouts '*puncture'* and as before, the others ride on.

She runs up to me pushing the bike. Lawrence gets out of the car and I grab the bike from Sinead and pass it to him. He adjusts the saddle and rides off up the road. Although Lawrence is quite small and built like a stick insect, he looks a bit awkward on her bike, but is already moving along pretty quickly.

Sinead is staring at me with her mouth open.

"Lawrence needs to stretch his legs a bit." I say. "He can ride at the same speed as you, so Mr Seymour won't be any the wiser when he's looking for you on his tracker. Sinead, you're out of it!"

I don't want to answer the bloody phone again. Sinead is still hugging me. She hasn't said much, but she's cried a lot. The tears are tears of relief.

It's the man from the Anti-Doping Agency wanting to know where the Trans-Global team are, but unfortunately I haven't got the faintest idea. I'm not quite as blunt as that, but have to admit that I'm not quite sure and explain that a friend is watching them at the moment. He doesn't sound impressed and somewhat pompously asks if I understand the importance of what I've been asked to do. When I tell him the person watching is an ex-policeman, he seems a bit more relaxed. I don't mention that he's seventy years old.

"Mike, can you talk - are you driving?"

"Yes, but I've got one of these hand-free ear thingies. They're useful when women call."

God, does he ever think of anything else?

"Where are the Trans-Global team?" I hold my breath.

"They're just coming out of Camelford. I'm about three hundred yards behind the support cars."

"Is there a black 4x4 with them?"

"I was wondering about him. Yes, he's sticking behind the support cars."

"And the motorhomes?"

"They came out of the camp behind the riders, but fell back and I had to overtake them. They might be behind, but I'm not sure."

The Agency guy sounds a lot more relaxed when I ring him back. I decide to wait until the Trans-Global team pass us and then see if the motorhomes are following.

Sinead listens quietly as I tell her about this morning's call with Sir Peter.

"If they want the drugs," she says, "they won't find them in any of the Trans-Global vehicles. They're much too smart. Everything's in Richard Seymour's Range Rover; hidden in loads of concealed hiding places."

"Well, let's hope he stays with Trans-Global and gets pulled in. I'm sure the Customs people will find them."

I don't know how long we'll have to wait for the team to go by and decide to use the time to gently find more out about Sinead.

"So where do you work?" I ask.

"Epsom Hospital, I'm a theatre sister."

"You don't work on the wards then?"

"Good Lord no. I've never been one for puffing up pillows and emptying bed pans. I like the operating theatre and all the technical bits that go with it. That's why Richard Seymour got to know me. He needed to get me on his side if he stood any chance of selling new instruments. Most surgeons will ask the nurse's opinion."

"So how well did you get to know him?"

"He's a smooth operator and spent loads of money wining and dining the surgeons and theatre nurses. It goes on all the time with people like him and pharmaceutical salesmen. It's a perk of the job. A year or so ago I drank too much one night and poured my heart out about the problems with my mother. That's how he guessed that I still needed money."

"You must need money pretty desperately to risk your career," I say.

"Oh believe me I do. I've lost count of the number of times I've re-scheduled her debts. As soon as I've done it, another one pops up to bite me. I was taking out loans just so I could pay the rent and feed us. Seymour worked his charm on me and made it sound so easy. I knew that I was taking a risk, but convinced myself that there was no way the College would find out. Even if they did, would they be bothered about a few tests for a sports drink? He said there was no way they could find out that I'd been paid."

Whilst she's been talking I've been keeping my eye on the wing mirror. The Trans-Global peloton comes into sight and in a matter of seconds have passed us. They are followed by the support cars and Seymour's car, with Mike a discrete distance behind. Mike doesn't notice my car and I think I can detect a smile on his face as he drives past. I suspect that this is the best time he's had in years where a woman isn't involved. Less than five minutes later the two motorhomes speed past and I drive off behind them. We have a convoy!

I ring the Agency man, tell him about the motorhomes and say that the riders are less than an hour away from Truro.

I know it must feel like another interrogation, but Sinead seems happy to answer my questions.

"I assume Seymour hasn't given you any money yet."

"He paid half up front. That was one of my conditions. I managed to clear most of the urgent debts and the second half was going to clear the lot, with a bit left over for a holiday."

"So you're going to have to pay him back." I say smiling.

"He'll be lucky, it's all gone. Oh and he bought me a nice new bike."

She snuggles down into the seat and closes her eyes. She's exhausted. I've got to admire her, she's ridden over nine hundred miles in eight days at a fast pace and has had to put up with so much stress and pressure. I just hope that it's all over for her.

Mike rings. The Trans-Global convoy has just joined the A390 and are about five miles away from Truro. He confirms that Seymour is still with them. I ring and tell the Agency man and am now his best friend. The motorhomes ahead of us are travelling quickly and the hills have slowed the Trans-Global riders, so we join the A390 not far behind Mike. The nearer we get to Truro, the more nervous I am about seeing Lawrence. He must keep ahead of Richard Seymour.

The road becomes dual carriageway as it bypasses the City Centre and I can see the Trans-Global riders ahead. It's safe to assume that the motorhomes are following the same route and so I overtake them. As we pass, my rear view mirror becomes full of headlights and blue flashing lights and as soon as I move back to the inside lane, a BMW police car goes past at high speed. After a roundabout the road sweeps up a long steep hill and the police car passes the Trans-Global support cars and riders and moves over in front of them.

The pit stop is on the left hand side at the crest of the hill and the police car drives past it. An illuminated flashing arrow pointing to the left streams across the bottom of the rear windscreen of the police car, which slows and stops at the entrance to a lorry park. The peloton of riders dutifully turn in, followed by the convoy of support vehicles. The 4x4 indicates left to follow them, but at the last moment swerves right around the police car, emitting intermittent puffs of grey smoke from the exhausts as it accelerates hard away. There are more puffs of smoke as Mike accelerates behind him. Oh my God, we've got a car chase with a septuagenarian pursuit driver!

It's pointless trying to keep up with them, so I pull into a lay-by and ring Mike's number.

The phone keeps ringing and finally connects to his voicemail.

"Mike, what the hell are you doing? Seymour's getting out, you can't follow him all the way to Dorking. Leave him to the police."

I hit the steering wheel in frustration. "Silly old sod. I should never have asked him to do it - he's going to kill himself."

Sinead touches my arm. "I think Seymour will try and dump the drugs he's got left. He won't want to be stopped with them in the car."

I realise that I must talk to Lawrence.

"Lawrence, it's Mark. Seymour didn't get pulled in. There's too much to explain now, but you've got to keep going, he'll still be tracking the bike."

As soon as I hang up, the phone rings. It's Mike.

"Where are you and where's Seymour?" I ask.

"He turned off the main road and he's now driven up a track into a small wood. It's too risky to follow him."

He explains roughly where he is and I drive for about a quarter of a mile and turn right into a small lane. After a few minutes I see Mike's car parked on the right hand side of the road and park about a hundred yards behind it.

My phone rings again and Mike says. "I can just about see him. He's parked up the track and is moving about, but he's too far away to see what he's doing."

"I'll bring the binoculars," I reply.

It's the fastest hundred yards I've run for a long time and I collapse into the passenger seat of Mike's car. He grabs the binoculars and focuses them on the track.

"Shit," he says. "He's reversing back, get back to your car. I'll turn into the track and make it look like I've stopped for a kip."

Great plan Mike and then what?

I can now see the 4x4's reversing lights about seventy five yards away and jump out of the car. The hundred yards back is the fastest I've run since three minutes ago.

My 'U' turn isn't quite perfect due to the appalling lock on the people carrier's steering and we bump over the rough grass verge before heading back to the main road. Almost opposite the junction is a petrol station and I pull in and park in one of the shopping parking spaces. I'm still out of breath and sweating.

Now what? We should probably have stayed where we were and just ducked down out of sight, but my natural instinct was flight rather than fight or perhaps it was the need to get Sinead out of the proximity of Seymour. I decide that I prefer the second reason.

I'm watching the junction and see the 4x4 stop. It's not signalling and when the road is clear, it crosses into the petrol station and pulls up at the pumps. Shit!

Sinead has seen him and crouches down in the front passenger footwell. She whispers. "Tell Mike to go and look up the track. I bet he's dumped the drugs."

I ring Mike. "Where are you?" I ask.

He sounds dejected. "Where I was before. Seymour got really pissed off because I was blocking his way, so I had to let him out. I couldn't go after him immediately or he'd see me. And then... well.... I sort of bottled it."

"What on earth do you mean?" I ask.

"I suddenly thought that I shouldn't be doing car chases at my age. I've still got far too much to do to kill myself now. I'm really sorry Mark."

"Mike," I say. "You've done exactly the right thing."

I tell him to drive back up the track to where Seymour stopped and prompted by Sinead, ask him to look for white boxes containing phials of clear liquid. I stress the importance of finding them and can sense the adrenalin flowing back into him.

This gets more bloody exciting every minute!

Seymour filled the 4x4 with diesel, but instead of driving back to Dorking, he's parked one space away from us and talking on the phone. To make matters worse the car that was between us has now driven off. I've turned my back to him the best I can and Sinead is still crumpled up in the footwell complaining of severe cramp. I think about driving off, but don't want to take the chance that he'll recognise me. He can't possibly be on the phone for much longer.

Mike rings sounding elated. "I've got them. Three boxes were hidden beneath branches and leaves in the ditch."

As I congratulate him, Sinead understands and despite her cramped position, raises a fist in celebration. I tell Mike where we are and I'm about to tell him to stay where he is until

Seymour goes, when I hear his car start up in the background. He then hangs up. I'm worried - what's the hell is he going to do now?

Five minutes later Mike is carefully reversing into the space between the people carrier and Seymour. I try to ring him, but my instincts are right and he doesn't answer. He keeps the engine running and smiles mischievously at me.

"What the fuck are you doing?" I mouth at him.

Mike doesn't respond.

He's blipping the throttle and watching the exit to the petrol station.

He then holds up a white box against the side window next to Seymour and sounds the car horn. As Seymour looks towards him, Mike holds up a single finger and smiles. Blue tyre smoke fills the air as the Impreza leaves the forecourt. Mercifully, there is a small gap in the traffic which Mike takes and the tyres squeal as he blasts his way towards Truro.

Seymour has to reverse if he is to follow Mike. He half completes the manoeuvre before presumably realising that he has no chance of catching him and drives back into the parking space. Sinead is desperate to know what's happening and I decide that it's time to leave. I know I shouldn't, but I can't resist the urge to look across at him. His naturally ruddy face is crimson and the veins on his temple resemble a tube map. I'm not really sure what a sick pig looks like, but it must be something quite similar. As I move off, he looks across towards me and I sense a slow dawning of recognition. There is of course only one sensible course of action - I hold up a single finger and smile.

The tyre smoke from a lowly people carrier is quite impressive.

Afternoon....

We meet up with Mike in the car park of a large supermarket on the Truro by-pass and I introduce him to Sinead. He eyes her up and down.

"Well Mark didn't tell me that you were so beautiful, it's no wonder he wanted to help you,"

he says.

Hands off granddad - I saw her first.

"Well Mike, not many seventy year olds get involved in a car chase," I say.

He laughs mockingly. "Call that a chase? It must have been all of a couple of miles. Still, he didn't realise I was behind him, so maybe I haven't lost it."

Sinead says, "I wouldn't fancy chasing him in a car, he's a bloody mad driver. He nearly killed us on the way to John O'Groats by passing a coach totally blind."

Mike looks at me quizzically and I realise that I hadn't totally filled in all of the gaps in the story.

"Was he the bastard who..."

I interrupt. "Yes Mike, so you got your own back."

"If I'd have known, I'd have....I'd have..."

I leave him deciding what he'd have done by interrupting again and saying that we need to make a move.

We haven't seen any more of Seymour and hope that he's now on his way back to Dorking with his tail behind his legs. The only reason he'd have for going to Land's End would be to make sure that Sinead was okay and we unanimously agree that such a chivalrous gesture would be totally alien to Seymour. Sinead had never planned to travel back with him and he'd bought her a train ticket which she won't be using - I'm not letting her out of my sight.

I ring Gillian and she sounds terrible. She and Bob have just arrived at the pit stop and the final hill has really taken it out of her. We agree that we'll try and meet up in Penzance.

Mike wants to follow the ride route up to the north coast and then down to Penzance. I've had enough of weaving in and out of cyclists and decide that we'll drive southwards through Penryn and Helston and then on to Penzance. It also means that if Seymour is still about, we stand more chance of avoiding him.

The last thing we do before we part is transfer the three boxes of drugs to my car. I think Mike has done quite enough for today.

I can tell that Sinead is tired, but she seems happy to talk, which is just as well as there are so many more things to ask her.

"I assume that enough samples were taken from the Trans-Global riders for them to know whether this drug works."

"Probably," she replies. They'll only miss out on the last samples from today, but that's not the point.

"What do you mean?"

She indicates towards the boxes in the back of the car. "Now that we've got these, it makes the drug almost worthless. The whole thing is a game of cat and mouse between those who manufacture or want to use the drugs and the drug testing agencies. Once they've been able to analyse what Trans-Global were using, they'll know what they're looking for and develop their tests so they will be able to identify it in the future."

"No wonder Seymour looked pissed off."

"Oh yes. He's lost an awful lot of money today."

I can see lines of worry on her face and gently squeeze her leg.

"Don't worry. He thinks you're still riding to Land's End. There's no way he can possibly link you with this."

"That's what I keep telling myself, but he frightened me - still does."

I don't want to admit that I share her nervousness and try hard to sound unconcerned.

"Don't worry," I say. "I'm here to protect you now and if I can't, I know a lecherous seventy year old who would love to step in."

I'm about to ask another question when she butts in.

"Right that's it! My turn. I want to know all about my knight in shining armour, starting with your ex-wife."

We're the other side of Helston when I finish my potted life story and I have to admit to being impressed. I'm sure she's not, but I am.

"My turn again," I say. "So what about your husband? I know he was a professional cyclist and his name was Danny - the same as you son."

"Now who's being doing their homework? Yes, we met when I was a semi-pro. We were young, I got pregnant and we got married. In that order. All the first born boys in his family had to be called Danny.

"How long did it last?"

"For a couple of years. I had to give up cycling and resented being cooped up all day when he was cycling all over the world. We also could never agree on drugs."

"Drugs? What do you mean?"

"Danny was quite happy to do whatever the team wanted, whether it was blood transfusions, EPO's or steroids. You name it he did it. He justified it by saying that everyone else was doing it and he couldn't be competitive if he didn't. The truth was that he wasn't quite good enough and used the drugs as a prop."

"What's EPO?" I ask.

"It's short for Erythropoietin. It's made by the body to control the number and capacity of the red cells in blood. But they've now developed synthetic alternatives which are used to enhance performance."

"How do they do that?"

"They increase the number of red cells which carry oxygen to the muscles or allow the red cells to carry more oxygen. Before they developed synthetic EPO, teams used blood transfusions to replace the rider's blood with super oxygenated blood, but that was difficult to do in hotel rooms and led to the riders getting very nasty infections."

"You didn't approve of Danny doing this sort of thing then?" I ask.

"No, I joined a pro-team for a while before I got pregnant and they put a lot of pressure on me to take them. I'd hit a bit of a ceiling at the time and it was tempting, but I said no and was gently eased out of the team."

"Does Danny have anything to do with Danny Junior?"

"Not really. He scratches a living out of doing a bit of commentary for Irish television and writes a few articles for the trade press and cycling magazines. He drinks too much and when he does come and see Danny it's usually a disaster. I'm sure that's why Danny's got no interest in cycling."

For the last few miles before Penzance we drive in comfortable silence.

We find a small cafe in Penzance which is slightly away from the front, but we can see the stream of cyclists passing the end of the road. A cup of tea triggers withdrawal cravings and I go up to the counter of the cafe. They can only partially satisfy me with a chocolate fudge bar and the woman serving looks bemused when I ask her if they've got any salami sticks.

Mike rings to tell me that he's with Gillian and Bob. They've stopped in Marazion just outside of Penzance because Gillian couldn't go any further without a rest. Bob and Mike are obviously having to work hard to keep her going. Mike has offered to drive her nearer to the finish, but she's obstinately refusing, saying she'd rather give up than cross the finish line without having ridden the whole way.

It's forty five minutes before we meet them on the promenade in front of the sad-looking nineteen thirties open air Jubilee Swimming Pool. Gillian isn't talking. She doesn't respond to my cheerful encouragement and I sense that the last fifteen miles might just as well be one thousand and fifteen miles.

Sinead and I leave them to drive towards Land's End and immediately reach Newlyn. I thought that Newlyn's only claim to fame was that the sea level datum was taken from there, but I realise there's another - the most difficult hill of the whole ride. Not only is the gradient in places about twenty per cent, but the road is narrow, twisty and busy.

A third of the way up I see a space where I can park and pull over. I look up and down the hill. There's no way Gillian's ever going to be able to do this. What idiot decided that this would be a good idea after nearly a thousand miles?

We get out of the car and wait. I can see the crossroads at the start of the hill and a few minutes later Gillian and Bob start to climb. Bob is already pushing hard out of the saddle, but I watch as Gillian's legs turn slower and slower. She's about fifty yards away when they stop altogether. She doesn't have time to release her feet from the pedals and falls sideways into the road. A car coming down the hill sees her and manages to stop in front of her. Sinead and I run down the hill towards her.

As we get closer Sinead says. "Leave this to me, it doesn't need two of us."

The car driver has got out of his car and is helping Gillian to the side of the road. He then picks up her bike and leans it against a lamp post.

Bob has stopped further up the hill and I turn and walk back up to him. I urge him to go on, trying to convince him that we can sort out Gillian and he reluctantly agrees. He clips one shoe into a pedal and pushes down for all he's worth and just manages to get enough momentum to move off.

I look on helplessly as Sinead comforts Gillian who's sitting on the kerb with tears streaming down her face. Sinead has wiped the blood away from a large graze on Gillian's knee with a tissue. If there's ever a time when she needs a bit of help from her husband's boss, it's now.

Mike has parked on the other side of the road and comes over. Sinead finally helps Gillian stand up and then collects her bike. Sinead holds the bike whilst Gillian gets back on. I can't hear what Sinead is saying, but she's giving some kind of instruction to Gillian who clips in one foot and moves the pedal almost to the top. Sinead grabs the seat post, holds the bike upright and shouts 'PUSH'. Gillian pushes down hard on the pedal, moves forward about eighteen inches and then stops by putting her other foot down on the ground. They repeat this half a dozen times and Gillian gets a little further each time. It reminds me of a father teaching a child to ride by taking off the stabiliser wheels. Sinead then tries to get Gillian to use her other foot, but each time she tries, her foot slips off the pedal and if it wasn't for Sinead holding the seat post she would have fallen again.

Sinead pulls out a small multi-tool from her jersey pocket and asks Gillian to take off her right shoe. Sinead unscrews the metal cleat on the underside of the shoe which clips into the pedal and hands the shoe back to Gillian.

"That should make it easier. You can't clip in, but your foot shouldn't slip so much," Sinead says.

Gillian looks at Mike and I and actually smiles. "I told you that I was going to ride every inch of this bloody ride."

Without the cleat, Gillian manages a couple of turns using both feet and with Sinead steadying her, inch by inch, foot by foot, yard by yard, Gillian makes it to the top where Bob is waiting.

More hugs, woman hugs and man hugs - anybody would think that it's the finish!

There's a direct way to Land's End from Penzance along the A30. I've no idea if it's got any hills, but can only assume that it hasn't and therefore didn't appeal to the sadistic mind of the route planner. Instead, we follow the B3315 which turns out to be a mini-mountain pass that meanders its way through tiny and unremarkable villages. For most of its length I drive alongside Gillian with Sinead hanging out of the window shouting *'breathe, push, come on you can do it'*. If I didn't know otherwise, I'd be convinced that Sinead is a midwife and not a theatre sister.

Finally, we make it to where the road meets the A30 and after another hundred yards we get to the crest of a hill and look down on the glory of

Land's End. It comprises a jumble of unremarkable white buildings and some equally unremarkable scrubland leading to the sea. It's as if someone has moved John O'Groats a thousand miles.

I pull off the road and Mike parks behind me. Shortly afterwards Gillian and Bob ride up and stop. Gillian is a ghostly white colour, but a quick glance at her chest assures me that blood is still coursing through her. We can see the finish bouncy castle rocking in the breeze and the metal barriers to funnel you through to the finish line. Even though we must be amongst the last to finish, there still seems to be quite a crowd of people to welcome riders.

I notice that Gillian and Sinead have gone to the back of the car. They return a few minutes later pushing Lawrence's bike.

Sinead pushes it towards me. "We've decided that you are going to have one last ride."

"You mean to the finish?"

"Yes, all of you. But, I think I should stay here, she says."

I ring Lawrence. He's at the finish waiting for us and I tell him to ride back and meet us. Five minutes later he's with us.

I turn to Mike. "Come on Mike, we're going for a ride, but don't worry - it's all downhill."

I can't believe that the crowd don't spot that two of the five cyclists riding side by side towards the finish are wearing ordinary clothes. They wave and cheer and we wave back. As we approach the line, Mike and I brake and let Gillian, Lawrence and Bob go ahead. Then Lawrence and Bob brake and Gillian sails over the line with her fist raised and punching the air.

Evening....

I'm sitting in the bar of the hotel in Penzance where I'd booked a single room some months ago. *Luckily?* They had a room for Sinead and I'm waiting for her to have a shower and get changed.

After going over the finishing line, we'd ridden back to Sinead and said our goodbyes. I've never had so many hugs and I'll admit to a few tears - okay a lot of tears. I know on these occasions you make promises to keep in touch and pledges to meet up again, but this time I really think that we all mean it.

Sir Peter has just rung and said that samples had been taken from the riders for testing, but without the actual drug, they'll struggle to detect it. Seymour had been stopped near to Salisbury Plain, but nothing was found in his car. I tried to picture Sir Peter's face when I told him that three boxes of the drug were safely stored beneath the bed in my room. I realised that I should have told him earlier, but felt no guilt. I'd had more important things to deal with. We'd agreed that he would make arrangements for the drugs to be picked up by the Agency the next day and in return, I promised I'd tell him just how I'd managed to be in possession of them. Finally, I'd reminded him of his suggestion that Haskin might like to sponsor a talented race driver.

Sinead joins me. Wow! She does scrub up well.

I pick up my jacket to get my wallet and feel something in the lining. There's a hole in a pocket and I retrieve a crumpled blue packet - moist wipes.

Sinead grabs them and smiles. "Moist wipes - you'll need those later."

At last I know what they're for. Perhaps I should have bought more packets.

Night...

Mind your own business - this ~~is~~ was a book about a bike ride!

About the Author

David Ward took early retirement from his career as a Chartered Surveyor and has since concentrated on cycling and writing. He has two grown up children and lives in Hertfordshire with his wife, Liz, who is a teacher.

He's twice successfully completed the annual Deloitte Ride Across Britain from John O'Groats to Land's End in 2010 and 2011.

It's All Downhill is his first published novel. A second novel, *A Letter at Christmas* is planned for publication in the first half of 2012.

Lightning Source UK Ltd.
Milton Keynes UK
UKOW040404261012

201227UK00001B/16/P